As he'd watched a flush of rose pink spread down her throat and across her décolletage, Carlos had wanted to reacquaint himself with her tantalizing contours.

He could not remember wanting anything so badly in his life.

When he had been tipped off about a story in the British tabloids that he had a secret child, he hadn't believed it for a minute. He could have instructed his lawyers to investigate. But for two years he'd been unable to get Betsy out of his mind, and if he was honest, he'd seized the excuse to meet her again. He had felt confident that his inexplicable fascination with her would end once he saw her and realized that she was nothing out of the ordinary. And when he had proof from a paternity test that she was a liar, he would be able to dismiss her as a mistake from his past.

But she was the mother of his son. He had received the confirmation email from the DNA clinic an hour ago and it reinforced his determination that Sebastian would not be illegitimate. To claim his son, he must marry Betsy.

Chantelle Shaw lives on the Kent coast and thinks up her stories while walking on the beach. She has been married for over thirty years and has six children. Her love affair with reading and writing Harlequin stories began as a teenager, and her first book was published in 2006. She likes strong-willed, slightly unusual characters. Chantelle also loves gardening, walking and wine.

Books by Chantelle Shaw

Harlequin Presents

Reunited by a Shock Pregnancy
Wed for the Spaniard's Redemption
Proof of Their Forbidden Night
Her Wedding Night Negotiation

Secret Heirs of Billionaires

Wed for His Secret Heir

Wedlocked!

Trapped by Vialli's Vows

Bought by the Brazilian

Mistress of His Revenge
Master of Her Innocence

The Saunderson Legacy

The Secret He Must Claim
The Throne He Must Take

Visit the Author Profile page
at Harlequin.com for more titles.

Chantelle Shaw

HOUSEKEEPER IN THE HEADLINES

Recycling programs
for this product may
not exist in your area.

ISBN-13: 978-1-335-14895-7

Housekeeper in the Headlines

Copyright © 2020 by Chantelle Shaw

This edition published by arrangement with Harlequin Books S.A.

For questions and comments about the quality of this book,
please contact us at CustomerService@Harlequin.com.

Harlequin Enterprises ULC
22 Adelaide St. West, 40th Floor
Toronto, Ontario M5H 4E3, Canada
www.Harlequin.com

Printed in U.S.A.

HOUSEKEEPER IN THE HEADLINES

For Rosie and Lucy, my amazing, adventurous and inspirational daughters who are true Harlequin Presents heroines. Love you. Mum xxx

CHAPTER ONE

'Is it true?'

'Of course it's not true.' Carlos Segarra scowled at the newspaper in his hands and swore. He looked at his father and recognised the expression of disappointment on Roderigo's face. *Dios*, he had given his father plenty of reasons to be disappointed with him over the years, Carlos acknowledged grimly. But *this* was something else, and he was innocent of the claim that had been made against him.

'I do not have a secret love child,' he said grittily. 'The story in the tabloids is a complete fabrication.'

Roderigo's breath wheezed in his chest. He had been lucky to survive a stroke a year ago, and a bout of pneumonia had put him back in hospital for the past month. 'So, you don't know this woman, Betsy Miller, who is alleged to be the mother of your son?'

Carlos's gut clenched as memories he should have forgotten after all this time surfaced. Pansy-brown eyes and hair a shade somewhere between caramel and golden honey that fell in silky curls around a pretty, passion-flushed face.

He remembered the moist softness of Betsy's lips and her husky moans of pleasure when he'd made love to her. She had tested his self-control for weeks, and that night two years ago—the night after he had achieved his dream of winning the men's singles title at the world-renown British International Tennis Championships—his control had shattered spectacularly.

'I knew her briefly in London,' he said stiffly. 'But I am not the father of her child.'

Roderigo gave him a close look. 'You are one hundred percent certain?'

'*Si.*' Carlos stared at the photo of Betsy on the front page of the newspaper. Even though she was wearing a shapeless raincoat and her hair was hidden beneath an unflattering woollen hat, he felt a sizzle of heat in his blood. The strength of his reaction was perplexing. He had never had a hang-up about any woman, ever. And he did *not* have one about an unsophisticated, English housekeeper, he assured himself.

'There is virtually zero possibility that the child is mine,' he insisted. The photo showed Betsy holding a child who looked to be a similar age to Carlos's nephew. The toddler's features were obscured by the hood of his coat.

If Betsy *had* fallen pregnant by him, why would she have waited until now to make it public? Carlos brooded. Why wouldn't she have told him first? Surely, a more likely explanation was that she had lied to the newspapers and been paid for her story.

Carlos recalled that circumstances had meant he had left the house where he had been staying in southwest London without seeing Betsy again after they had spent the night together. But he'd been unable to forget her, and a few weeks after he had returned to Spain, he'd sent her a gift of a bracelet, as well as his phone number, and suggested that she could call him if she wanted to meet him again. She had not replied, and he hadn't tried to contact her again. Carlos did not chase women, and usually he did not have to. But if Betsy had conceived his baby, he would have expected her to get in touch with him and at the very least ask for financial support for the child.

'This is simply another form of a kiss-and-tell story that the tabloids love to print,' he told his father as he threw the newspaper down on the bed. 'There are women who deliberately sleep with a well-known figure and then sell the story to the press.'

'If you had not earned a reputation as a playboy, perhaps this woman would not have targeted you.'

The disapproval in Roderigo's voice irritated Carlos. He thought of the annexe that he'd had built onto his house in Toledo to provide his father with private living accommodation. Carlos paid for Roderigo to receive round the clock care from a team of nurses instead of having to move into a nursing home. He had hoped that by offering his father a home, they might be able to re-establish their relationship which had once been close.

He did not expect forgiveness. How could he, when he would never forgive himself for the part he had played in his mother's death? But he had sensed a softening in Roderigo's attitude towards him in recent months. Carlos had hoped for a rapprochement between them, but the story in the newspaper was damning, and his father's lack of faith in him felt like a knife in his ribs.

He rose from the chair next to his father's bed and paced restlessly around the hospital room. 'What will you do?' Roderigo asked.

'My jet is being prepared to take me to England immediately after I leave here.' It was sheer coincidence that Carlos had planned a business trip to the UK. Ironically, he had considered getting back in touch with Betsy, reasoning that if they had an affair, his fascination with her would undoubtedly fade. Now he was determined to track her down, and his first priority was to contact a DNA clinic to arrange a paternity test.

He wanted answers, and when he had proof that Betsy Miller was a liar, he would make her regret that she'd made a fool of him, Carlos vowed in silent fury.

The river had burst its banks during the night. June had been unseasonably wet, and a month's worth of rain fell in twenty-four hours, turning the pretty stream that meandered through the Dorset village of Fraddlington into a raging torrent.

Betsy had piled sandbags around the front door of the cottage, but in the morning she discovered that the floors of the downstairs rooms were submerged beneath inches of filthy brown water—although fortunately the kitchen at the back of the house had been built on a slightly higher level and remained dry. The water had gradually drained away but it left behind a thick layer of black silt that stunk.

Sebastian stood behind the child gate that Betsy had fixed across the doorway between the kitchen and the sitting room. He was nearly fifteen months old and utterly adorable. His brown eyes were flecked with gold, just like his father's eyes. But Betsy refused to think about Carlos.

'I'm afraid you will have to stay there while I clear up this mess,' she told her little son as she leaned down and kissed his dark brown curls.

Betsy rented the cottage and had no idea where she and Sebastian could go while the flood damage was repaired. The village had been on high alert to the possibility of the river bursting its banks for several days, and news crews had flocked to Fraddlington to report on the unfolding situation. When she dragged a sodden rug outside and dumped it in the front garden, she saw her neighbour talking to a man holding a microphone.

Betsy went back inside and shut the door, thinking about another journalist who had approached her a few days ago while she had been pushing Sebastian in his buggy. She had suddenly realised where she had seen the journalist before.

Two years ago, he had come to her aunt's house in south-west London to interview Carlos Segarra, that year's winner of the men's singles title at the British

International Tennis Championships, widely known as the BITC. Betsy had been working as the housekeeper there, and Carlos had leased the house for several weeks during the tournament while Aunt Alice had gone abroad.

After spending the night with Carlos, Betsy had woken late the next morning and, finding herself alone in his bed, had gone to look for him. She had ached in places she'd never ached before, and the lingering proof of Carlos's intimate caresses had made her long for him to make love to her again.

Memories of that night pushed into her mind. What a naive fool she had been, she thought bitterly as she pushed the mop across the floor and wrung a stream of muddy water into a bucket.

Growing up in the war zone of her parents' toxic marriage and their acrimonious divorce had made her sceptical about the idea of falling in love. She had been on a few dates with guys she'd met at university, but she'd never had a serious romantic relationship because she was fearful of lowering her barriers and risking being hurt. And yet deep down she had still cherished a hope of meeting her prince—and he had arrived in the form of a tall, bronzed and impossibly handsome tennis star.

For the only time in her life Betsy had let her guard down, with Carlos, believing that there was a special connection between them. But the truth was that she had been just another notch on his crowded bedpost. She had overheard him telling the journalist who had come to the house to interview him about his success that she was 'a casual fling'.

Peeling off her rubber gloves, Betsy felt a surge of despair as she glanced around the cottage. She had enough to worry about without the sense of foreboding that had gripped her since she'd recognised that journalist in the village. She was sure that he remembered her from two years ago, and it made his curiosity about Sebastian unsettling.

A knock on the front door made her jump. It was probably someone from the emergency services, checking on the residents who had been affected by the floods, she told herself. She looked in the kitchen and saw Sebastian sitting on his playmat. There was another loud knock and she moved towards the front door. Through the frosted glass pane she could make out a tall figure, and inexplicably her heart started to thud.

'Hi…' Betsy's voice faltered as she opened the door—and stared at Carlos.

Shock turned the blood in her veins to ice. It *couldn't* be him. He did not know where she lived and there was no reason why he would be looking for her. No reason that he would be interested in anyway.

She had forgotten how gorgeous he was. Not that she'd been able to forget him at all. But Carlos Segarra in the flesh was a thousand times more devastatingly handsome than the man who regularly haunted her dreams.

Her eyes roamed his hard-boned features, taking in his masculine beauty; the razor-edged cheekbones above the hollow planes of his face, the square jaw shadowed with dark stubble, and the mouth that she knew could be sensual or cruel, but right now was drawn into a grim expression that made Betsy's heart sink.

Carlos's stunning looks and his fame as a superstar sporting legend, not to mention his reputation as a prolific playboy, meant that he often featured in celebrity magazines. Betsy hated herself every time she succumbed to her curiosity and bought a magazine that had a picture of Carlos, dubbed 'Spain's sexiest man', on the front cover. But she had been irresistibly attracted to him the moment she'd set eyes on him two years ago, and now she was dismayed to discover that his impact on her had not lessened.

She felt a quiver in the pit of her stomach as her gaze locked with his sherry-gold eyes, gleaming beneath thick, dark lashes.

It wasn't only his eyes that made her think of a jungle cat. She pictured the lean, muscular body, honed to physical perfection, that had made him a superb athlete. On the tennis circuit he had been nicknamed 'The Jaguar', because of his speed around the court and his unpredictability. You could never know what a jaguar was thinking, and the same went for Carlos Segarra.

Swallowing hard, Betsy ran her eyes over Carlos's elegant grey suit. The bottom few inches of his trousers were damp and his brown leather shoes were caked in mud. 'You should have worn boots.' She bit her lip when she realised that that was an odd way to greet him after two years. 'Why are you here?'

His heavy brows snapped together. 'I have only just arrived in England and I was not aware of the floods that have affected this part of the country.'

His accented voice sent a shiver of response across Betsy's skin. She could feel the pulse at the base of her throat hammering and lifted her hand to hide her traitorous body's reaction to him.

Carlos's hard gaze flicked over her shapeless tee shirt and faded sweatpants. She'd dressed in old clothes, knowing that she was bound to get filthy in the clean-up operation. He glanced down at her mud-spattered wellington boots and his mouth flattened. Betsy resisted the temptation to remove the scarf that she'd tied over her hair. She looked a mess, but she did not give a damn what Carlos thought of her, she assured herself.

'The flooding has been a big story in the media. I'm surprised you haven't read about it.' She looked at the newspaper he was carrying under his arm. 'If you had it might have saved your suit.'

'To hell with my suit.' Carlos's tone was blistering. 'Are you trying to be funny?'

She blinked. 'What do you mean?'

He thrust the newspaper into her hand and stepped into the cottage without waiting for her to invite him in.

'Dios...' he muttered as he glanced around the sitting room. There was a brown tidemark halfway up the cream sofa, and an unpleasant smell permeated the

room. 'I'm guessing that this flood damage will be expensive to repair. Is that why you did it?' he demanded.

'Did what? I don't understand.' Betsy backed away from the lethal gleam in Carlos's eyes. He was clearly furious. Once again she felt a sense of foreboding.

She looked at the front page of the newspaper. It was one of the more lurid tabloids and her heart slammed against her ribs as the headline leapt out at her.

Tennis Ace Segarra's Secret Son!

There was a photo of Betsy, standing in front of the cottage holding Sebastian. The picture was rather grainy, and her son was wearing a rain suit with the hood up so that his face was mostly obscured.

She immediately thought of the journalist who had carried sandbags up the garden path and helped her pile them against the door.

'You don't mind if I take a photo, do you?' he'd asked. 'I'm writing a piece about the floods for the local rag and the editor likes to include pictures showing the human element of the story.'

Betsy had felt she couldn't refuse, seeing as he had helped her. The journalist had then casually asked Sebastian's age and commented on his olive complexion. But she was sure she hadn't said anything which would have led him to guess that Carlos Segarra was her baby's father.

'I have no idea how this story got into the papers,'

she said shakily. 'I've never told anyone that Sebastian is yours.'

Carlos snorted. 'Of course you know. How much did you get paid for this garbage that has been printed which accuses me of abandoning my child?'

'I didn't—' She broke off as Carlos slashed his hand through the air with an impatient gesture.

'Last night I received a tip-off that the story that I had a secret love child was about to break in the British tabloids. I was too late to seek a legal injunction to prevent the story being published,' he said tersely. 'My informant said that the "scoop" had been uncovered by a scumbag journalist called Tom Vane, who believes he has a score to settle with me because he blames me after he was sacked from his job as a sports reporter. He wrote a load of lies about my reasons for retiring from playing competition tennis and I complained to the newspaper he worked for.'

'I don't know the journalist's name,' Betsy muttered. 'He was hanging around the village a couple of days ago and he told me he worked for a local newspaper. He seemed familiar and I remembered that I'd seen him once at my aunt's house in London.'

Carlos's jaw hardened. 'Do you expect me to believe you?' he asked sardonically. 'It's obvious that you and Vane devised this story that I have a secret child. I suppose he promised you that the tabloids would pay you a fortune if you said that I am the father of your baby? But you won't get away with it. I want a paternity test.

And when I have proof that the child isn't mine, I will sue you for libel.'

Betsy had often tried to imagine Carlos's reaction if she told him about his son. Sebastian was growing up fast and was already developing a cheeky personality. It had saddened her that his father would never know him. Her conscience had pricked. Maybe she should have given Carlos the chance to decide if he wanted to be involved with Sebastian. But he had just given a TV interview in which he'd stated that he had no desire to settle down and have a family. Betsy had taken that as proof that he would not be interested in his son. And besides, she'd had no way of getting in touch with Carlos after he had returned to Spain.

She supposed that she could have tried to contact him through his management company, but she hadn't because her deepest fear had been that Carlos might decide that he *did* want Sebastian and try to take the little boy from her. Betsy knew what it was like to be at the centre of a custody battle. Her parents had fought over her, and she had felt torn between them. She was determined to spare Sebastian the same ordeal.

Now she felt relief at Carlos's reaction, which confirmed what she'd guessed: fatherhood held no appeal for him. But his accusation that she had sold her story to the newspapers made her furious.

For a moment, she contemplated denying that Sebastian was Carlos's son. Then he might go away and leave her in peace. But if he carried out his threat to sue her for libel the truth was bound to come out.

She lifted her chin and met Carlos's angry glare proudly. 'A paternity test will prove that I am telling the truth. Sebastian *is* your son.'

Carlos was taken aback by Betsy's vehement response, but he reminded himself that she was bound to stick to her claim that she'd had a child by him. Surely she must realise she wouldn't get away with making such a false accusation.

'We spent one night together, and I used protection both times we had sex,' he said curtly. 'Frankly, it would have been a miracle if you had conceived my baby.'

She nodded. 'I don't know how it happened, but I agree that our son is a miracle.' She walked across the room to where a gate was fixed in the door frame and held out her arms. 'Isn't that right, poppet? You are Mama's little miracle.'

Carlos stiffened as he watched a small child walk unsteadily over to the gate and lift his arms to Betsy. She picked him up and balanced him on her hip.

'This is Sebastian.'

There was fierce pride in her voice, and the look of love in her eyes as she smiled at the baby evoked a tug in Carlos's chest. A long time ago his mother had smiled at *him* with the same loving pride.

He pushed the memory away as he stared at the little boy, who had big brown eyes and a halo of dark curls and bore a striking similarity to Carlos's nephew. His sister's son, Miguel, was two, and he guessed that

Betsy's child was a few months younger—which meant that she must have fallen pregnant around two years ago.

'He's yours,' Betsy said quietly. 'He's almost fifteen months old. He was born on the seventeenth of April, exactly nine months after you and I slept together. Before you suggest that I could have slept with another man at around the same time—I didn't. I was a virgin and I haven't been with anyone since you.'

It was impossible, Carlos assured himself.

He was conscious that his heart was pounding as hard as if he'd played a five-set tennis match. The fact that this child bore a resemblance to his nephew proved nothing. Sebastian could have inherited his brown eyes from his mother.

But when Betsy walked towards him, carrying her son, Carlos discovered that the little boy's eyes were the tawny colour of light sherry and flecked with gold—exactly like his own.

Something close to panic gripped him. He *couldn't* have a child. He'd spent his entire adult life avoiding responsibility.

His mind flew back to two years ago. He had been at the peak of his career; winner on the international tennis circuit more times than any other player. But the London tournament's coveted gold trophy had eluded him. It was the one victory he'd wanted above all others and his driving ambition had been to win the tournament in his mother's honour.

He had rented a house in London close to the tennis

club, where he trained for a few weeks before the start of the tournament. But his determination to avoid distraction and focus on his game had been tested when an attractive young brunette had greeted him.

'I'm the housekeeper, Betsy Miller,' she'd introduced herself with a shy smile. 'Don't worry,' she'd assured him quickly when he had frowned. 'I promise that you won't notice me around the house.'

Her skin was pale cream and the rosy flush that had spread over her cheeks had snagged his attention. His initial opinion that she was simply attractive fell far short of the truth, he'd realised. This housekeeper was pretty in a wholesome, fresh-faced way that he'd found unexpectedly sexy.

She was petite, and her figure was slim rather than fashionably skinny. His eyes had been drawn to the firm swell of her breasts before he'd dropped his gaze to the narrow indent of her waist and the gentle flare of her hips.

Returning his eyes to her face, he had watched her blush deepen and recognised awareness in her expression. It happened to him so often that he was never surprised. He was rarely intrigued by a woman. But something about Betsy had stirred his jaded libido.

'Don't be too confident of that promise,' he'd murmured. 'You are *very* noticeable, Betsy Miller.'

Dios! Carlos forced his mind back to the present in this flood-damaged cottage. The woman standing in front of him looked like a character from a Dickensian novel in her filthy old clothes and with her hair hidden beneath a scarf. But even though Betsy wore no make-up, and lacked the glamour and sophistication of his numerous past mistresses, her natural beauty and innate sensuality lit a flame inside him.

To his astonishment, he felt his body spring to urgent life. Why her? he wondered furiously. He'd gone through a rocky period after he'd won the BITC, and his libido had fallen off a cliff. In fact, he hadn't slept with any other woman since Betsy.

The startling realisation did nothing to improve his temper.

'I have never had a condom fail before,' he said harshly. 'And if by a minuscule chance it did, why didn't you tell me when you found out you were pregnant?'

'I didn't know until a few weeks after you had gone back to Spain.' She bit her lip. 'I saw you being interviewed on television, soon after you had announced your retirement from competition tennis. After there had been rumours in the media that you planned to marry your girlfriend, the model Lorena Lopez, and start a family.'

Carlos gave a snort. 'I had a brief affair with Lorena, but it was over before I went to England to prepare for the championship. I had made it clear that there was never a chance I would marry her, but she wouldn't accept it and told the press that we were engaged.'

Betsy nodded. 'You told the TV chat show host that you were a "lone wolf" and did not intend to ever marry or have children. I realised then that you wouldn't want your baby.'

It could not be true.

Carlos raked his fingers through his hair. When he'd seen that newspaper headline he had been certain the allegation that he had a secret son was untrue. Now he did not know what to think. Betsy was either a very good liar or she was telling the truth, and the child who was struggling to wriggle out of her arms was his flesh and blood.

'Poppet, I can't put you down on the dirty floor,' Betsy murmured, trying to pacify the little boy, who had started to grizzle.

Sebastian might only be fifteen months old, but he was already showing signs that he was strong-willed. *Had he inherited the trait from* him? Carlos wondered.

'I have arranged for a paternity test to be carried out,' he said abruptly. 'A doctor is waiting at a hotel a few miles from here to take the necessary samples and the DNA testing clinic guarantees the result in twenty-four hours.'

'What do you intend to do when the result is positive?' Betsy challenged him. 'If you plan to regard Sebastian as merely your responsibility, or worse an inconvenience, it might be better not to do the test. You can walk away right now and forget about him.'

'Is your reluctance because you know the test will prove you are a liar?' His jaw hardened. 'You have publicly alleged that I am your child's father and I am determined to clear my name.'

Angry spots of colour flared on her cheeks. 'I swear that the story in the tabloids had nothing to do with me.'

'It couldn't have happened at a worse time.' Carlos could not hide his frustration. 'This evening there is a party in London to launch the UK office of my sports management company. Veloz represents some of the biggest names in the world of sport. But now my integrity is being questioned. I want the truth, and a paternity test is the only way I can be sure to get it.'

'Fine.' Betsy did not drop her gaze from his. 'I'm all for the truth. But how can we go anywhere while the village is flooded? I'm surprised you were able to get here.'

'I came to Fraddlington by helicopter and walked across a field as the main road is impassable.' Carlos strode towards the front door, grimacing as his hand-crafted Italian leather shoes squelched in the layer of mud on the floor. 'Let's go.'

'You obviously know nothing about small children if you think I can simply leave the house.'

Betsy's wry voice stopped him.

'I'll need to pack a change bag for Sebastian and make up a bottle of his formula milk.'

The toddler had stopped squirming in her arms and was staring at Carlos. He was a beautiful child. Carlos was once again struck by Sebastian's resemblance to his nephew.

He walked back to Betsy, compelled by a feeling he could not explain as he studied her son's apple-round cheeks and mop of dark curls. 'I'll hold him while you organise what you need,' he said tersely.

She hesitated. 'He might not want to go to you. He's wary of strangers.'

Carlos held out his hands and took the unresisting little boy from her. He had some experience, having been coerced by his sister to hold his nephew since Miguel had been a tiny baby.

The strong similarity between the two boys *could* simply be coincidence, he assured himself. He was not going to jump to conclusions ahead of the DNA test. Nevertheless, he felt an unnerving sense of recognition when his gaze locked with Sebastian's sherry-gold eyes.

Betsy had asked what he intended to do if he had proof that he was her baby's father. Up until he'd walked into the cottage he had not seriously considered it a possibility. But she sounded so certain that he had to accept it might be true. And if it was…if Sebastian was his…

A host of conflicting emotions surged through Carlos, but the fiercest and most unexpected was protectiveness. Since he was a teenager he had not had the support from his own father that he had desperately wanted, and he had even doubted that Roderigo loved him. If Sebastian *was* his, he would claim his son and love him unconditionally.

CHAPTER TWO

BETSY HELD HER breath as the helicopter took off. After the torrential rain that had caused the floods it was a beautiful sunny day and there was not a cloud in the blue sky.

'Are you nervous about flying?' Carlos was sprawled in a seat opposite her in the luxurious cabin and appeared totally relaxed, unlike Betsy.

'I'm not a fan,' she admitted, and gasped as the helicopter jolted.

'That was just some turbulence.'

His gravelly voice sent a shiver of sexual awareness across Betsy's skin and she knew the knot of tension in her stomach had nothing to do with her nervousness about being in the helicopter.

She couldn't quite believe that Carlos had turned up at the cottage. If only she'd had prior knowledge of his visit she might have been able to erect some defences against his smouldering sensuality, but instead she felt like a teenager on a first date.

'Have you flown in a helicopter before?' he asked.

'Not since I was a child and visited my father. He had a pilot's licence and lived in a remote part of Canada which was only accessible by helicopter.'

'Why didn't you live with him?'

'My parents divorced when I was eight and my mother was awarded custody of me, but the access arrangement stipulated that I could spend time with my dad.'

Betsy looked away from Carlos and stared out of the window as memories crowded her mind. After the divorce she had lived with her mother in London, but every school holiday she'd been put on a plane to Toronto to visit her father. Towards the end of one visit, Drake Miller had driven her to a small airfield where they had boarded a helicopter.

'We're going to have an adventure,' he'd told her. 'Just you and me, exploring one of the wildest areas of Canada.'

'Is Mum okay with it?' Betsy had felt uneasy. 'I have to go back to England before school starts next week.'

'The truth is, honey, that your mother doesn't want you living with her any more.' Drake had frowned when she'd started to cry. 'Hey, what are your tears for? Don't you want to be with your old dad?'

Of course she did, she had quickly assured him as she'd scrubbed her tears away. She'd loved both her parents. But she thought she must have done something terrible for her mum to have sent her away permanently.

Six months later the Canadian police had arrived at the log cabin in a remote part of British Colombia where Betsy had been living with her father and she'd learned the truth. Drake had kidnapped her. He had lied when he'd said that her mother did not want her. He'd maintained that he had done it because he could not bear to live apart from his only daughter. But Betsy suspected that he'd kept her hidden out of spite, as part of his festering feud with her mother.

Her childhood had left her with a deep mistrust of the concept of romantic love, and she could not understand why she had fallen under Carlos's spell so completely. What she'd felt had been lust, she reminded herself. And that was certainly all it had been for Carlos.

After she had overheard him telling the journalist that she was a casual fling, she'd written him a note, making the excuse that she'd had sex with him because he was famous and telling him that to avoid any awkwardness it would be better if they did not see each other again. Then she had left the house, and when she'd returned, hours later, he had gone.

Sebastian was growing bored with sitting still and tried to wriggle off Betsy's lap. She was conscious of Carlos's brooding gaze, watching them, and wondered if he was judging her parenting skills.

Motherhood had been a steep learning curve for her, especially as she'd had no help from anyone. Her mother had flown over from LA, where she now lived, when Sebastian was six weeks old, but Stephanie Miller had spent most of the visit telling Betsy that she did not feel old enough to be a grandmother and that it would be the end of her acting career if film producers discovered her real age.

Betsy had refrained from pointing out that her mother hadn't had a big film role for years. And after several glasses of wine Stephanie had admitted that she had money problems.

'I wish I could help you out, darling, but my finances are stretched. I expect your father is raking it in with the royalties from his books,' she said bitterly. 'Apparently, he's the top thriller writer in North America, although I'm surprised that he has the energy to write. His latest wife is only a year or so older than you.'

Betsy had not met her father's third wife. She'd been estranged from him since she'd fallen out with wife number two and Drake had told her it was best if she didn't visit again. She'd phoned him when Sebastian was born, and he'd sent a congratulations card, but he had never met his grandson.

'I don't need money from Drake,' she'd told her mother. 'My pet portrait business is doing quite well, and I supplement what I earn from painting with my job at the village pub.'

Now she doubted that she would be able to resume her job as barmaid. Her friend Sarah, who owned the pub, had said that it been badly damaged in the floods. And she would have to move out of the cottage, where she had a painting studio in the attic.

Sebastian started to grizzle, and Betsy stroked his curls off his brow. 'Not long now, poppet,' she said, trying to soothe him. She glanced at Carlos. 'How far is the hotel?'

He spoke to the pilot over the intercom, 'We'll be there in a couple of minutes.'

Carlos's sunglasses hid his expression and Betsy had no idea what he was thinking. When he had held Sebastian at the cottage she'd hoped for *something*—a sign that he recognised his son. Seeing Sebastian with his father had emphasised their physical likeness, but perhaps Carlos couldn't see it—or more likely he didn't want to accept the baby was his.

She wondered what his reaction would be when he had proof of paternity. His main concern seemed to be damage to his reputation, which might affect his business interests. But the news story would be forgotten in a few days.

And she had no intention of asking Carlos for financial support. Sebastian was her responsibility. She wasn't the first woman to have listened to her heart rather than her head and then had to cope with the consequences, Betsy thought ruefully.

Her stomach muscles clenched as she inhaled the evocative spicy scent of Carlos's cologne. Desire flared sweet and sharp inside her as her mind flew back to the night that she had spent with him.

The velvet sofa had felt sensuous against her skin as Carlos had eased her down onto the cushions. She hadn't been aware of him undressing her, or himself, until she'd felt the roughness of his chest hair on her breasts. His hands had been everywhere, working their magic on her breasts and skimming over her thighs as he'd parted her legs and tested her wet heat with his fingers.

She remembered how big and hard his manhood had felt when she'd touched him, and the nervous flutter of her heart when he'd pressed forward and entered her. He had filled her, completed her. And now the dampness between her legs was shameful proof that she only had to look at him and her body turned to mush.

She blushed when she realised that she was staring at him. She wished she could rip off his sunglasses to see if he was affected by the sexual chemistry that was almost tangible in the confines of the helicopter cabin.

A nerve flickered in his cheek—but perhaps she had imagined it. Carlos had dated some of the world's most beautiful women and he wouldn't be interested in *her*, Betsy reminded herself. He was gorgeous and exotic and so sexy he should come with a health warning.

'We're about to land,' he told her smoothly.

Get a grip, she ordered herself a few minutes later as she followed him across the helipad in the grounds of his hotel. The impressive country house was *the* place to stay in Dorset. Betsy had changed out of her old leggings before leaving the cottage, but when she walked into the elegant foyer of the hotel she was conscious of the receptionist's disapproving glance at her jeans and strap top.

Carlos led her over to the lift, which whisked them up to the penthouse suite. There, a doctor was waiting to take cheek swabs from all three of them.

After carrying out the simple procedure, the doctor left. Carlos's phone rang and he went into the bedroom to take the call.

Sebastian was due for a nap, but he wasn't ready to give in and protested loudly while Betsy changed his nappy. She searched in the change bag for his favourite toy but couldn't find it, and in desperation emptied the bag over the floor.

Carlos walked back into the room as Sebastian's screams reached a crescendo. 'What's the matter with him?'

'He's tired,' Betsy said shortly. 'And I must have left his cuddly toy rabbit at the cottage.'

'Surely if Sebastian is tired he will fall asleep without the toy,' Carlos said, in a dry tone that exacerbated Betsy's frustration and the feeling that she was a useless mother.

Her fierce awareness of Carlos did not help. He had changed out of his suit and muddy shoes into black jeans, a black polo shirt and a matching leather jacket. He quite simply took her breath away.

'What do you know about childcare?' she snapped, raising her voice above Sebastian's yells.

Exhaustion was catching up with her after a sleepless night spent listening to the river flooding into the cottage. It was sinking in that she was homeless, Sebastian was crying because he wanted the familiarity and security of falling asleep in his cot, and Betsy felt close to tears as she wondered what she was going to do.

'Perhaps if you calmed down Sebastian would stop

crying?' Carlos murmured. 'He is probably picking up on your tension.'

'It's your fault that I'm tense.' Betsy glared at him. 'I feel violated.'

He frowned. 'How so?'

'I found it humiliating to have a stranger take samples from me and Sebastian for DNA testing,' she said hotly. 'You and I might have only spent one night together, but I was your housekeeper for six weeks and we got to know each other fairly well. I thought we had become friends.' She bit her lip. 'What makes you think I would lie about you being Sebastian's father?'

'Everything I believed I knew about you went up in smoke when I found your note saying that the only reason you'd had sex with me was because I was famous,' Carlos said tersely.

'I wrote that note after I overheard you telling the journalist who had come to interview you that I was a casual fling.' Betsy grimaced. 'Sebastian is the consequence of the night we spent together.'

'So you say,' Carlos drawled. 'The truth will be confirmed in twenty-four hours. I intend to stay in London tonight. You and Sebastian can stay here as you can't sleep at the cottage. There is a cot in the bedroom. I'll be in touch tomorrow.'

'I can't wait,' Betsy muttered sarcastically as she swept past Carlos and carried Sebastian into the bedroom.

He had worn himself out with crying and was asleep almost as soon as she laid him in the cot.

When she returned to the sitting room Carlos had gone, and she was angry with herself for feeling disappointed. He made her feel alive in a way that no other man had ever done, she acknowledged with a sigh. She dragged her thoughts from him, knowing that she needed to make long-term plans.

Her landlord had called to say that he intended to sell the cottage, and a trawl on the internet of estate agents' websites showed there was nothing suitable in the local area that Betsy could afford to rent. She would be lucky to find a place with enough room that she could set up a studio, she realised as she read the details of a poky basement flat.

She thought of the picture that she had worked on recently. The portrait of a golden Labrador had been commissioned by a client as a birthday present for his wife. The painting was finished, and she needed to arrange for it to be delivered to the client. The money she would be paid for the painting was even more vital now, as it would be a while before she could accept any more commissions.

Betsy switched on the television and watched a local news report that told her the floodwater around Fraddlington had receded and the main road was open again. Maybe she would be able to go back to the cottage to collect Sebastian's cuddly toy and pack up the painting.

'We're going to go on a bus,' she told him when he woke up from his nap.

Although he didn't understand, he gave a grin that showed off his two new teeth and Betsy's heart melted.

But when she carried him out of the hotel, they were immediately surrounded by press photographers.

A journalist thrust a microphone towards her. 'Miss Miller. Is tennis legend Carlos Segarra really your son's father?'

'How long have you been in a relationship with Carlos?'

'Is it true that you had sex with Segarra on a famous London tennis court?'

'Of course it isn't true,' Betsy denied angrily.

She clutched Sebastian tightly as the press pack swarmed closer. He was whimpering and pushing his face into her neck.

'Please let me pass,' she appealed to the photographers. She felt like a rabbit caught in a car's headlights as camera flashbulbs went off all around her.

'Miss Miller, if you would like to come with me?'

Betsy turned towards the calm voice amid the chaos and saw a smartly dressed man pushing through the crowd of paparazzi.

'I'm Brian Waring, the manager of the hotel,' he introduced himself as he slipped a hand beneath her arm and led her quickly back inside the hotel.

To Betsy's relief, the photographers did not follow.

The manager escorted to the lift. 'Might I suggest that you remain in the hotel and its grounds, where you will not be troubled by the press? Mr Segarra has asked me personally to ensure that you and your son have everything you need.' He gave a kindly smile, perhaps realising that Betsy was still too shocked by what had happened to be able to speak. 'I'll arrange for lunch to be served in your suite.'

She bit her lip. 'I don't know how the press found out I was here.'

'The paparazzi are renowned for using underhand methods in their pursuit of a story,' the manager murmured. 'I believe that the tabloid newspapers are prepared to pay thousands of pounds for a picture of a celebrity or someone close to them, especially if there is a whiff of a scandal.'

So her little son was a scandal!

Perhaps she would wake up and find that this day from hell was simply a nightmare, Betsy thought when she and Sebastian were safely back inside the hotel suite. The incident with the photographers had left her badly shaken and had brought back memories of the intrusive media coverage of her father's trial after he had been accused of abducting her.

She shuddered at the thought that now her name was in the public domain the media might dig up the story of her parents' famously acrimonious divorce. Neither her mother nor her father had seemed to care that their lives had become a soap opera, played out in regular instalments in the tabloids, but Betsy had hated the press attention on her family.

Her phone rang, and she stared at it suspiciously before breathing a sigh of relief when she saw that it was her friend Sarah who was calling.

'Betsy, I've just seen the headlines. We've been so busy clearing up the pub, and I hadn't looked on social media, but Mike popped to the shop and bought a paper…'

'It was the same for me,' Betsy said ruefully. 'The first I knew of the story was when Carlos arrived at the cottage and showed me a newspaper.'

'Oh, my goodness! What did he say about Sebastian?'

'He has demanded proof of paternity.'

'The thing is…' Sarah sounded strained. 'I think it's my fault that the story was published.'

'How do you mean?'

'You know how for the past few days we've been putting up defences in the hope of stopping the pub from being flooded? To be honest, saving the business that Mike and I have worked so hard to establish was all I could think about. Well, a journalist came into the pub and said he was covering the story now that the river was likely to burst its banks. He seemed a nice guy, and he offered to help move the furniture and carpets upstairs.'

Sarah sighed.

'I feel such an idiot for believing him when he said he was a friend of yours from London and he already knew that Carlos Segarra was Sebastian's father. If I'd been thinking straight I might have been more suspicious. Instead I said something along the lines that I thought it was about time Carlos accepted responsibility for his son. But when I saw today's newspapers I remembered that you had said I was the *only* person you had confided in. I'm so sorry, Betsy. Are you all right?'

'Not really.' Betsy explained what had happened when she'd tried to leave the hotel.

'The paparazzi are outside your cottage, too. Me and my big mouth,' Sarah muttered. 'But I'm sure that in a couple of days the press will forget the story and move on to something else,' she said consolingly.

But the damage had been done, Betsy thought heavily. Tomorrow Carlos would have proof that he was Sebastian's father, but he had given no indication that he would welcome the news.

The rest of the day dragged, as she tried to keep Sebastian entertained in the hotel suite that had become a prison. Luckily she'd packed spare clothes for him, as well as pouches of food and cartons of ready-made formula milk.

After she'd settled him in the cot for the night, she ran a bath and tipped a liberal splash of gorgeously scented bubble bath into the water. After a long soak, she wrapped herself in one of the hotel's fluffy robes and rinsed out her knickers in the bathwater.

Dinner was delivered to the room, but she felt too tense to eat. She had been jogging along nicely, but in the past twenty-four hours her life had imploded. She'd lost her home and her painting studio, and Carlos has stormed back on to the scene. But there was nothing she could do tonight, she thought wearily as she curled up on the sofa and tried to concentrate on a political thriller on the television.

Betsy woke with a start and for a moment felt disorientated before she remembered that she was in the hotel suite. Something had disturbed her, and she sprang up from the sofa. The television was still on—perhaps she had been woken by a sound from it. But her skin prickled as she sensed that someone was in the bedroom where Sebastian was sleeping.

Heart pounding, she ran into the bedroom and saw a figure leaning over the cot.

'Carlos?'

She let out a shaky breath and slumped against the door frame as he turned around and the soft light from the bedside lamp illuminated his handsome face.

'You scared me. I thought a photographer had managed to get into the room.'

Carlos frowned. 'Have the paparazzi been here?'

'There was a crowd of them outside the hotel earlier. I wanted to go back to the cottage, but they wouldn't leave me alone and Sebastian was frightened.' Betsy had spoken quietly, but Sebastian stirred. She held her breath and after a moment he settled again. 'What are you doing here?' she whispered to Carlos.

He stared down into the cot before walking across the room. She followed him into the sitting room, pulling the door closed behind them.

'I accept that Sebastian is my son.'

Betsy's heart lurched. 'I thought you wouldn't receive the result of the DNA test until tomorrow.'

'I haven't heard back from the clinic.'

'Oh!' She couldn't hide her shock. She felt as if a weight had lifted from her. But her pleasure that Carlos seemed to trust her was quickly doused.

'I cannot ignore the evidence. Sebastian bears a strong physical resemblance to me. I checked his birth certificate to verify his date of birth.' He gave her a sardonic look. 'You didn't think I would simply take your word, did you? I realise that Sebastian must have been conceived at the time I was in England for the tournament.' Carlos's eyes glittered with fury. 'I will *never* forgive you for keeping him from me. I had a right to know that I am his father.'

His words tugged on emotions that Betsy did not want to feel. Deep in her heart she knew that she should have tried to contact Carlos when she'd discovered she was pregnant. But he had abandoned her after he'd slept with her in London and she had felt foolish because she'd trusted him. He was no better than her father, who had seemed to want her but had abandoned her in favour of his second wife.

'You publicly stated that you didn't want children,' she said to Carlos defensively. 'I was suffering from awful morning sickness when I watched you being interviewed, and I was convinced that you wouldn't want your baby.'

He said something in Spanish that she guessed from his savage tone was not complimentary. 'You should have told me instead of playing judge and jury. Sebastian has two parents, but you have deliberately deprived him of his father.'

A voice from the past slid into Betsy's mind and she recalled the words of the judge who had presided over her father's trial when he'd been charged with abducting her.

'You deliberately and cruelly deprived your daughter of her mother,' the judge had told Drake.

But the situation between her and Carlos wasn't the same as her parents, she tried to reassure herself. Her father's behaviour had been driven by a desire to hurt her mother. Betsy had kept Sebastian a secret from Carlos because… Had she subconsciously wanted to punish him for returning to Spain after he'd taken her virginity and crushed her heart?

She swallowed hard, unable to face the uncomfortable thoughts swirling in her head and unwilling to meet Carlos's hard gaze.

'What do you want?' she asked huskily.

'My son.' His tone was grim and uncompromising. 'Sebastian is a Segarra. You have stolen the first fifteen months of his life, but from now on his home will be with me in Spain.'

CHAPTER THREE

'ARE YOU THREATENING to take Sebastian away from me? You have no rights to him.'

Carlos heard fear in Betsy's voice and saw her mouth tremble before she quickly firmed her lips. But the sign of her vulnerability did not lessen his anger. *Dios—* 'angry' did not come anywhere near to describing the bitter betrayal he felt. He had a child, a son.

But Betsy hadn't told him.

'I am determined to be fully involved in my son's life,' he said harshly. 'I have already spoken to my lawyer who has advised me that when I have proof of paternity I can apply to the court for a Parental Responsibility Order, which will give me the right to be included in decisions made about Sebastian's upbringing.'

Betsy's shocked expression gave Carlos a stab of satisfaction. *See how she likes having the ground ripped from beneath her feet,* he thought.

His common sense had urged him to wait for the result of the paternity test. But in his heart he had known that Sebastian was his when he'd held the toddler in his arms at the cottage.

It wasn't only their physical similarity, and the fact that Sebastian bore a close resemblance to Carlos's nephew. The connection he felt with Sebastian was on a fundamental level—as if his soul had recognised the blood bond between them.

While he had been at the Veloz party in London his conviction that the little boy was his had intensified. Launching his sports management agency in England had been Carlos's focus for months, but he'd made an excuse to his business partner and left the party early to rush back to Dorset.

'I'm…glad that you believe Sebastian is yours.'

Betsy did not sound glad—she sounded as if she'd swallowed glass.

'I won't object if you want to be part of his life, and maybe when he is older he could spend holidays with you in Spain. But his home is in England, with me.'

'Your home will be uninhabitable for many weeks until the flood damage is repaired.'

Carlos frowned as he pictured the poky cottage where Betsy had been bringing up Sebastian. Had a lack of money driven her to tell the press that she'd had a child by him?

He had retired from the international tennis circuit two years ago. But he had dominated the game for over a decade and still played exhibition matches around the world. The paparazzi's fascination with his private life showed no sign of lessening and the tabloids must have paid thousands of pounds for the story.

'No doubt you were paid well by the tabloids for the revelation that I am Sebastian's father,' he said grimly. 'But I guarantee that what you received was a tiny fraction of my personal fortune. Sebastian is entitled to the lifestyle and benefits that my wealth can provide. I own a beautiful house in Toledo, where he will be able to thrive, and I can give him opportunities far beyond anything you can offer him.'

Betsy stared at him. 'Sebastian is my world. I can give him everything he needs, and his needs are simple. Love, safety and security—not a big house and a bucketload of cash.'

The belt of her robe had loosened, causing the front to gape open slightly, giving Carlos a tantalising view of the pale slopes of her breasts. He was infuriated by his body's instant response as a jolt of electricity arced through him and centred in his groin. He was still at a loss to understand why this woman, pretty but not in the supermodel league, made his skin feel too tight and his pulse quicken.

He wanted to hate Betsy for what she had done. He told himself that he did. But he could not resist stepping closer to her.

She smelled divine. Her hair was loose, tumbling in soft waves around her shoulders, a delicious mix of honey and caramel shades. Her brown eyes were wary, and her mouth was set in a sulky line that tempted him to crush her lips beneath his and kiss her until she made those soft moans in her throat that he still remembered.

Two years ago he had decided that she was too young and unworldly for him—especially while he needed to focus on preparing for the tennis tournament in London. His inconvenient attraction to a star-struck ingénue who seemed refreshingly unaware of her allure had been something Carlos had been determined to ignore. He'd almost succeeded.

But it had been impossible to ignore Betsy completely when she made his breakfast every morning and prepared dinner for him every evening.

It was ridiculous for them to eat separately, he'd told her after the first week, and he'd insisted that they dined together. With sex off the table—although he'd had several erotic fantasies in which he made love to her on the polished walnut surface of the dining table— he'd had to fall back on conversation. And not the kind of small talk he usually made with women as a prelude to taking them to bed.

His discussions with Betsy had covered a wide range of subjects, although he hadn't talked about his family and nor had she, except to tell him that the house belonged to her aunt and she combined her housekeeping duties with studying for an art degree.

In the tournament's final he'd played the best tennis of his life. And when he'd held the trophy aloft it had felt like a dream. But his euphoria had been tinged with guilt, because he had known his ferocious ambition had destroyed his family. His father's absence from the supporters' box had hurt.

Carlos had smiled for the photographers and kissed the trophy, but in his heart he would have gladly exchanged his success for his mother's life.

That evening he'd left the competitors' ball early and had felt dangerously out of control as he'd raced back to Betsy. He'd needed an outlet for the wild emotions that he hadn't been able to deal with.

Sexual chemistry had simmered between them for weeks, and when he'd pulled her into his arms that chemistry had ignited as fast as a Bunsen burner.

Carlos swore beneath his breath as he forced his mind from the past. Jaw tense, he strode across the hotel room to the minibar. The whisky was a blended variety, not his preferred single malt, but it would do.

He glanced at Betsy. 'Would you like a drink?'

'Why not? I could do with some Dutch courage,' she said, in a wry voice that tugged on something deep inside Carlos. Despite his fury, he disliked the idea that she might be afraid of him.

He half-filled two glasses and sensed without turning around that she had walked over to him. Her bare feet made no sound on the plush carpet, but his senses were assailed by her scent: something lightly floral, mixed with the vanilla fragrance of her skin, that made his gut clench.

He handed her a drink and led the way over to a sofa and chairs which were grouped around a coffee table. Lowering himself onto the sofa, he gave her a sardonic look when she made for the armchair furthest away from him. She took a sip of whisky and spluttered.

Two years ago Carlos had found her lack of sophistication refreshing, but now he could not decide if her unworldly air was real or if she had ruthlessly manipulated the media.

As if she had read his thoughts, she said quietly, 'The journalist who came to the village must have remembered that he had seen me with you at my aunt's house. It was a long shot that he guessed that Sebastian is your son. He found out that I worked at the pub and told the landlady there that he and I were friends in London and that he knew you are Sebastian's father. Sarah unthinkingly confirmed it because she was distracted by the threat of the flood.'

It was possible that Betsy was telling the truth, Carlos conceded. The antipathy between him and Tom Vane after he'd been instrumental in the journalist being sacked from his job had escalated further when Vane had threatened to make public some details he'd discovered about Carlos's mother's death. But the blackmail attempt failed when Carlos had informed the police.

'Even if what you say is true, how could the pub landlady have confirmed to Vane that I am Sebastian's father?' he asked coldly.

A scarlet stain spread over Betsy's face. 'Sarah is my closest friend…and I confided in her.'

Carlos swore. 'When I showed you that tabloid headline you assured me that you hadn't told *anyone*.

Clearly that was another lie. Did you not think I had
the right to be informed that I have a son?' he gritted.
'I should have been the first to know, instead of discovering from a goddamned newspaper that I am a father.'

'*How* could I have told you? Either when I found out
I was pregnant or after Sebastian was born? You went
back to Spain the day after we had slept together and
I had no way of contacting you.'

'That's not true. I included my phone number and
an invitation to visit me in Spain with the bracelet I
sent you.'

Betsy stared at him. 'What invitation? What bracelet?'

He frowned. 'Are you saying that you did not receive
a package? It was addressed to you, and I received no-
tification from the courier that it had been delivered
to your aunt's house.'

'I never heard from you again after you left and,
frankly, I don't believe you sent me anything. You're
making it up so that it doesn't look like you abandoned
me.'

'*You* are accusing *me* of lying?' Carlos couldn't believe what he was hearing, and his temper simmered.

'It doesn't feel good, does it?' Betsy said coolly.

His jaw clenched at her belligerence, but he felt a reluctant respect for her. Two years ago Betsy had been
star-struck and in awe of him, but motherhood had
turned her into a lioness determined to protect her cub.

Was she lying when she insisted that she hadn't
received the bracelet? Carlos raked a hand through

his hair, frustrated by this unexpected turn of events. Betsy's surprise seemed genuine. Her accusation that he had abandoned her would make more sense if she had not received his gift.

He had been piqued by her lack of response, and hadn't tried to contact her again. But that did not excuse her failure to tell him he had a child.

He welcomed the resurgence of his anger. It was safer to feel furious than to admit to himself that he longed to open her robe and trace his hands over her delectable curves. The idea that she was naked beneath the robe was a distraction he was struggling to ignore.

'I am willing to believe that you did not sell out to the tabloids,' he said curtly. 'In some ways I suppose I should be grateful that the story has broken. Would you have *ever* told me about my son?'

She bit her lip. 'I don't know. I wanted to, but I didn't know how you would feel. When you came to the cottage this morning your reaction was exactly as I feared.'

It had not been his finest moment, Carlos acknowledged. His shock when he'd seen Sebastian had been mixed with something close to fear. He knew his failings. His first thought had been that he wasn't up to the task of being a father. More importantly, that he did not deserve to have a child. Panic had gripped him, and he'd rejected the idea of such a huge responsibility.

But Sebastian was his. And maybe, Carlos brooded, this was his chance to atone for the past and his mother's untimely death.

Inside his head, Carlos heard his father's voice. *'You*

killed her. Mi querida Marta.' Tears had streamed down Roderigo Segarra's face.

The horror of that day would never leave Carlos, nor would his father's condemnation of him. It was the reason he had isolated his emotions from everyone—even his sister, who had been just a child when she had been made motherless. By him.

Panic seized Carlos once again. He did not deserve to be part of his baby son's life. What if he destroyed Sebastian like he had destroyed everything else that was good and pure? It would be better—safer—if he bought Betsy a house in England and gave her a generous allowance so that she could be a full-time mother to Sebastian.

His conscience pricked at the idea that she struggled financially. 'Who looks after Sebastian while you work at the pub?'

'When he was a small baby I used to leave him asleep in his pram in a room behind the bar. He was perfectly safe,' Betsy said when Carlos frowned. 'But he's too big to do that now. Luckily Sarah's sister offered to babysit on the evenings I worked. Polly can get on with her homework because Sebastian usually sleeps soundly. Unless he's teething,' she added ruefully.

'*Homework?* How old is this babysitter?'

'She's fifteen, and very responsible.' Betsy glared at him. 'I have always done the best I can to keep a roof over our heads and Sebastian clothed and fed. And working behind the bar in the evenings means that I have a couple of hours during the day when Sebastian has a nap to build up my pet portrait business.'

'Your—*what*?'

'I paint portraits of people's pets. Dogs and cats, mainly, but I've done a few rabbits—and a bearded dragon. Admittedly, I don't earn a fortune, but the business is starting to grow.' She sighed. 'The flooding means that I won't be able to accept any new commissions. My studio is in the attic, but I'll have to move out of the cottage and I don't know where or when I'll be able to paint again.'

Betsy sipped her whisky and wrinkled her nose. She looked very young, wrapped in the too-big towelling robe. But she must be in her mid-twenties, Carlos thought, and she possessed an inherent sensuality that he found irresistible. He could not prevent his gaze from straying to that enticing glimpse of her cleavage and he swore silently as his body tightened and his blood pulsed hot in his veins. Desiring the mother of his child was a complication he did not need when there was something far more important to be resolved.

Hearing how Betsy had struggled to bring up Sebastian on her own, leaving him in the care of a schoolgirl while she went to work, had filled Carlos with horror. As for painting pets—it might be a nice hobby, but Betsy couldn't seriously expect to make a living from it.

'I can solve all your problems,' he said coolly.

She looked at him warily. 'How?'

Carlos was aware of the powerful beat of his heart. Since his mother had died, he'd avoided all responsibility and commitment. He had lived up to his public persona of a playboy because that way no one expected anything of him, and no one got hurt. But this was too big and too important for him to run away from.

He had a son, and he would not allow Sebastian to grow up feeling rejected by his father the way Carlos had felt rejected by his own father.

'Marry me.'

He ignored Betsy's shocked gasp.

'If you agree to be my wife, I will take care of you and our son and your worries will be over.'

'Of…of course I'm not going to marry you,' Betsy stammered when the shock that had seized her released its stranglehold on her vocal cords.

Carlos's proposal had sounded more like an order, and she was in no doubt that he did not want *her*. Astonishingly, he *did* want his son.

'In the twenty-first century people don't get married because they have a baby.'

'I do. I *will*.' His voice was hard, implacable, and Betsy's heart collided with her ribs when she realised that he was only controlling his temper with ferocious will power.

'I won't allow my son to be illegitimate,' he told her. 'And before you say that it doesn't matter—it does. Sebastian should have *my* name on his birth certificate, and he should not be denied the name Segarra or his Spanish heritage.'

'You're crazy.'

Fear churned in the pit of her stomach. Carlos sounded as if he meant it. As if he actually expected her to marry him.

'I don't want to get married. I have no objection if you want to have a relationship with Sebastian—'

Carlos cut her off. 'How can I trust that you won't disappear with him? Once we are married and my name is included on Sebastian's birth certificate we will share equal parental rights.'

'Have I hurt your pride? Is that what this is about? You can't simply waltz into Sebastian's life when you feel like it and disappear again when you find that fatherhood doesn't suit your playboy lifestyle. Details of which are documented in unedifying detail in all the gossip magazines,' she added caustically.

'I'm flattered that you obviously take a close interest in my personal life.'

Beneath his mockery, the sting in his voice warned Betsy that he was furious.

'I don't want access rights to my son, or occasional visits. I want to see him every day and tuck him into bed every night.' His voice deepened. 'It is important to me that as Sebastian grows up he knows I'll always be there for him and will support him whatever happens.'

Despite herself Betsy felt a tug on her emotions in response to Carlos's statement, which sounded like a holy vow. She was stunned that he was prepared to go to such extreme lengths—even marry her—to claim Sebastian. But his talk of marriage brought back memories of her parents screaming abuse at each other. She would not risk her little boy having the kind of fractured childhood that she'd had.

The sound of crying from the bedroom gave her an excuse to drop her gaze from Carlos's and she put her drink down and sped across the room.

Sebastian's flushed cheek was a sure sign that he was cutting another tooth. Betsy picked him up and tried to soothe him.

'There's some teething gel in his change bag,' she told Carlos when he followed her into the bedroom.

He found the gel and she rubbed some onto Sebastian's gums, but his cries did not abate.

'Let me take him.' Carlos stretched out his arms and, after a moment's hesitation, Betsy handed the baby to him. 'Shh, *conejito*…' Carlos murmured, tucking Sebastian against his shoulder.

A lump formed in Betsy's throat at the sight of her little boy being comforted by his father. She realised that she could not deny Sebastian his daddy, nor Carlos his son. But she wouldn't marry him. No way.

'We'll talk in the morning,' Carlos told her when Sebastian had eventually fallen asleep and he'd laid him in the cot. 'You can sleep in the bed and I'll take the sofa in the sitting room.'

He left the room without glancing at her again, and Betsy let out a shaky sigh when he closed the door behind him. She felt physically and mentally exhausted and simply slipped off her bathrobe before she climbed into bed and sank into oblivion.

* * *

Sunlight was poking through the gap in the curtains when Betsy opened her eyes. For a few seconds she wondered where she was, but then memories crowded her mind: finding Carlos in the hotel suite, his acceptance that Sebastian was his, and his shocking marriage proposal.

Her watch showed nine o'clock. It was unusual for Sebastian to sleep so late. She looked over at the cot and her heart juddered to a standstill when she saw that it was empty. For a few seconds her brain struggled to comprehend the unthinkable.

Her baby had disappeared.

In sheer panic she leapt out of bed and ran across the room. As she wrenched open the door she told herself that Sebastian must have woken and Carlos had picked him up and taken him out of the cot.

But they weren't in the sitting room.

Terror swept through her as she remembered how Carlos had said that from now on his son would live with him in Spain. What if he had abducted Sebastian? How would she get her baby back? It had taken months for the Canadian authorities to find her when she had been kidnapped by her father.

Betsy choked back a sob. She could not bear to be parted from Sebastian for one day.

Her handbag was on the coffee table—and it was open. Before the cottage had flooded she had put her and Sebastian's passports, his birth certificate and other important documents in her bag for safekeeping. With mounting dread, Betsy rifled through the bag and discovered that the passports were missing.

She remembered that Carlos had said he had checked Sebastian's date of birth. She'd assumed he had looked online. Birth certificates were a matter of public record and available for anyone to see. But he must have opened her bag, found the birth certificate and removed the passports—which meant he could already have taken Sebastian abroad.

Fear cramped in Betsy's stomach.

When the door at the far end of suite opened and Carlos emerged from the bathroom, holding Sebastian, her knees sagged as relief swept through her.

'I woke up and…and Sebastian was missing.' Her voice shook. 'I thought you had taken him to Spain.' Anger replaced her fear and she glared at Carlos. 'Where are our passports?'

'I locked them in the safety deposit box,' he said calmly. 'You had left your handbag open and I noticed the passports and moved them. You shouldn't leave them lying around. All kinds of hotel staff have access to the suite.'

Carlos set Sebastian down on his feet and he toddled across the room and picked up a fluffy toy. 'You said that you had forgotten his favourite toy rabbit, so I bought him a replacement while I was in London.'

Betsy exhaled slowly as some of the tension drained from her body. 'That was kind of you.'

'Sebastian needed his nappy changed, but I thought

you might be disturbed if I took him into the en suite bathroom.'

She became aware that Carlos was staring at her, and her heart skipped a beat as she belatedly remembered that she had slept naked because she hadn't brought any nightwear with her to the hotel. When she'd leapt out of bed she'd been frantic to find Sebastian and hadn't thought to pull on the bathrobe.

Carlos looked as though he had been chiselled from marble, so still was he. His skin was drawn as tight as a drum over the sharp edges of his cheekbones and there was tension in the unforgiving line of his jaw. Beneath his heavy brows his eyes glittered, and Betsy's pulse quickened in response.

She remembered the one and only other time she had been naked in front of a man. This man.

Two years ago, Carlos had laid her down on the sofa and knelt over her, supporting his weight on his elbows while his gaze roamed over her body. When his eyes had returned to her face there had been a fierce hunger in his expression that had filled her with nervous excitement. She had been a virgin, and unprepared for the intensity of his unbridled passion.

He had marked her for ever when he'd made her his. She understood that now, and it made the ache in the pit of her stomach more intense, heavier, *needier*.

There was no mistaking the feral hunger in Carlos's eyes as he subjected her to a leisurely inspection, allowing his gaze to linger on her breasts before moving down to the slight curve of her stomach, the flare of her hips, and finally to the dusting of honey-brown curls between her thighs.

Heat scorched Betsy and a red stain spread over her cheeks. Her entire body felt on fire, and she burned hotter still when her nipples tingled and tightened, jutting forward as if begging for his touch, his mouth.

A lifetime passed, or so it felt, and the air between them throbbed with sexual tension. Betsy could not control the wild restlessness inside her, the fire that consumed her. She was transfixed by the golden gleam in Carlos's eyes, the hunger he could not hide.

Until he had turned up at the cottage she'd never expected to see him again. And since then he had been so angry that it hadn't occurred to her that he might find her attractive. But desire was stamped on his hard features and on his full, sensual lips, which for once were not curled in an expression of cynical contempt.

Moments ago she had been terrified that he had taken Sebastian to Spain. Now she was terrified that if Carlos kissed her she would be unable to resist him.

She crossed her arms over her breasts and blushed again when he gave her a sardonic look that said it was too late for modesty.

'I have to…' Her voice trailed away. She couldn't think straight while Carlos continued to stare at her as if she were prey and he was preparing to devour her.

But the spell was broken. He blinked, and when his thick black lashes lifted again his eyes were coolly dismissive.

'Hurry up and put some clothes on. We'll go to your cottage so that you can pack everything you and Sebastian might need before we fly to Spain today.'

CHAPTER FOUR

CARLOS RAKED HIS hands through his hair as Betsy spun round and raced back into the bedroom. His eyes followed the gorgeous rounded curves of her bottom and he did not know how he stopped himself from going after her.

When he'd walked into the sitting room and she had been standing there, completely and beautifully naked, he'd felt stunned. She was every bit as lovely as he remembered and then some. Motherhood had softened the angles of her body and given her a sensual allure that made him catch his breath. With her hair rippling in silky waves on her bare shoulders she'd reminded Carlos of a painting by one of the Old Masters.

She had been Aphrodite, or a Siren, and he'd wanted to worship her with his mouth pressed against her creamy skin. As he'd watched a flush of rose-pink spread down her throat and across her décolletage and lushly perfect breasts he had wanted to reacquaint himself with her tantalising contours. He could not remember wanting anything so badly in his life.

His mind flew back to two years ago. Betsy had been in the lounge at the house in London when he'd hurried back from the competitors' ball.

'Did you wait up for me?' he'd asked her.

'Of course I waited up for you.'

Her shy smile had floored him. He had wanted her for weeks, but he'd made himself wait for her to give him a sign. She'd walked over to him and wound her arms around his neck. When she'd drawn his head down and pressed her lips against his, the wolf inside him had howled.

He had been too impatient to take her upstairs to the bedroom and had tugged her clothes off before tumbling her down onto the sofa. The moonlight slanting through the blinds had cast a pearly shimmer over her nakedness so that she had seemed ethereal. He remembered the soft gasp she'd given as he'd cupped her breasts and licked her nipples. And when he'd slipped his hand between her thighs and touched her intimately she'd made a choked sound that he had thought was pleasure.

Could it have been surprise? Surely he would have known if she had been a virgin? But he had been so hungry for her, and intent on satisfying his desire, Carlos thought uncomfortably as he pulled his mind back to the present.

The previous day, when he had been tipped off about the story in the British tabloids that said he had a secret child, he hadn't believed it for a minute. He knew he could have instructed his lawyers to investigate. But for two years he'd been unable to get Betsy out of his mind and, if he was honest, he'd seized the excuse to meet her again. He had felt confident that his inexplicable fascination with her would end once he saw her and realised that she was nothing out of the ordinary. And when he had proof from a paternity test that she was a liar he would be able to dismiss her as a mistake from his past.

But she was the mother of his son. He had received the confirmation email from the DNA clinic an hour ago, and it had reinforced his determination that Sebastian would not be illegitimate. To claim his son, he knew he must marry Betsy. But it was disturbing to realise how close he had come to losing his self-control simply by looking at her.

Since he had lost his temper with devastating results when he was a teenager, Carlos had kept a tight hold on his emotions, and he never made rash decisions. But in the past thirty-six hours all that had changed—and Betsy was to blame, he acknowledged grimly.

Two years ago she had gotten under his skin in a way that no other woman had ever done, and she was having the same effect on him now. But, just because she made him feel like a callow youth with an overload of hormones, it did not mean that he was in danger of succumbing to his inconvenient desire for her, he assured himself.

He *could* handle her, and he *would* marry her for his son's sake. Sebastian was the innocent one in this messy situation that his parents had made.

It occurred to him that Sebastian was being unusually quiet. The reason became clear when he looked across the room and saw that the toddler had found the baby wipes in the change bag and was pulling them out of the packet. All around him the carpet was littered with wipes.

'Hey, *conejito*! That means little rabbit in Spanish,' he told his son as he hunkered down next to Sebastian and shoved the wipes back into the packet. 'We had better not tell your mama what you've done or we'll both be in trouble.'

No doubt Betsy would accuse him of failing to keep a close eye on the baby, Carlos thought ruefully.

Sebastian's lower lip wobbled ominously when he realised he could no longer play with the wipes. Carlos quickly handed him the new toy rabbit. Sebastian grabbed it and his rosebud mouth curved into a smile that would melt the steeliest heart.

Carlos sucked in a breath. He still couldn't quite comprehend that this angelic little boy was his son. His fingers shook as he brushed them over Sebastian's silky brown curls. He was utterly perfect and enchanting.

Carlos stood up and scooped the baby into his arms. The skin on Sebastian's cheeks was as soft and downy as a peach, and his black eyelashes were impossibly long and curling. He was unmistakably a Segarra—although Sebastian had his mother's button nose, Carlos thought, running his finger along his own nose, which had been described as 'aquiline' by a female fashion editor who had written gushingly about him in a magazine when he'd modelled a brand of sportswear.

Since he'd retired from playing tennis he'd felt adrift. Sure, he'd established his sports management agency, and was actively involved in running Veloz, but he had a superb team of executives and the reality, Carlos knew, was that he was just the figurehead of the company. His charity, the Segarra Foundation, was important to him, but in truth he had been struggling to find purpose in his life. What better purpose could he have than being a father to his son?

Sebastian's face was so close to his that Carlos could count his long eyelashes. He wondered if his own father had felt this overwhelming urge to protect him when *he* was a child. Carlos had been closer to his mother, but he'd had a good relationship with his father—until that fateful day—the day when he had destroyed his family. His father had never forgiven him.

A small finger poked into his eye made Carlos wince. 'Steady there, *conejito*,' he said softly as Sebastian continued to explore his face with chubby little hands. And then, quite unexpectedly, Sebastian pressed his mouth against Carlos's cheek and gave him a dribbly kiss.

Carlos had noticed that Betsy was demonstrative with the baby, and often kissed his cheeks, and there was no doubt that Sebastian was copying the affectionate gesture.

Dios! His heart clenched. *'Tu es mi hijo,'* he told Sebastian huskily. 'You are my son. I will take care of you and love you always.'

* * *

Betsy could not put off facing Carlos any longer. She had taken her time dressing, but she only had to put on her jeans and top and tie the laces on her trainers. Bundling her hair into a loose knot on top of her head had wasted another couple of minutes. Her reflection in the mirror revealed a hectic flush on her cheeks. She wished that instead of a skimpy strap top she could cover up with a baggy sweatshirt to disguise the betraying peaks of her nipples.

Her stomach muscles clenched as she recalled how Carlos's eyes had roamed over her naked body with a shocking possessiveness that had infuriated her. She wasn't *his*. But the hunger in his gaze had warned her that if Sebastian had not been in the room Carlos would have tumbled her down on the sofa and trapped her beneath him with a muscular thigh, just as he had done two years ago.

She was appalled by how excited she felt at the idea of him making love to her.

Taking a deep breath, she opened the door and sidled into the sitting room. While she had been hiding in the bedroom a breakfast trolley had been delivered to the suite. The aroma of ground coffee and freshly cooked toast assailed her, and she discovered that she was starving. Sebastian was sitting in a high chair and Carlos was feeding him yoghurt.

'Stop hovering,' he drawled when he glanced over at her. 'It wasn't the first time I've seen you naked.'

She might have guessed that he wouldn't be tactful and refrain from mentioning the embarrassing incident.

Flushing hotly, she marched across the room and sat down at the table. 'It's lucky the paparazzi can't see you now. It wouldn't do your playboy reputation any good if word got out that you are adept at nappy-changing and feeding a baby.' She gave him a puzzled look. 'I didn't expect you to be so at ease with Sebastian.'

'I've had plenty of practice with my nephew. My sister has a two-year-old son,' Carlos explained as he fed Sebastian a spoonful of yoghurt. 'Graciela gave birth the night after I'd won the championship. She said that the tension of watching my match on TV brought on her labour.'

He grimaced.

'Miguel was born with a heart defect that required emergency surgery a few hours after his birth. My sister was in pieces when she called me. Her husband is a naval officer, and his ship was on a tour of Antarctica, and our father is mostly confined to bed or wheelchair-bound after he suffered a stroke a year ago. I rushed back to Spain the morning after you and I had spent the night together to be with Graciela.'

Betsy believed him. It wasn't likely that he'd make up a story about his nephew needing life-saving surgery.

'It must have been so frightening for your sister.'

She remembered how overwhelmed she'd felt when the midwife had placed Sebastian in her arms moments after he'd been born. He had seemed fragile, even though he'd been a strong, healthy baby.

'You mentioned your father, but not your mother,' she said carefully. Perhaps Carlos's family was as splintered as hers.

'She's dead.' His voice was emotionless. 'She died when I was fourteen and Graciela was ten. My sister grew up without her mother, and it was hard for her—especially when Miguel was ill, and she was so worried about him. She needed support from her family.'

Something about Carlos's closed expression stopped Betsy from prying into his mother's death. 'Was Miguel's surgery successful?' she asked.

'Thankfully, yes. He is a normal, active two-year-old.'

Carlos watched Sebastian munch on a finger of toast that Betsy had given him.

'The first time I saw my nephew he was in a neonatal unit and attached to various tubes and wires that were keeping him alive.' A muscle in his jaw clenched. 'It put my victory into perspective. I had won the trophy I'd coveted, but it seemed meaningless when my sister's baby's life hung in the balance.'

'Did it have anything to do with your decision to retire from playing professional tennis?'

Betsy had been as shocked as Carlos's legions of fans when he'd announced that he would not be defending his BITC title nor playing any more tournaments.

He nodded. 'I'd achieved everything I had set out to do playing tennis.'

Once again his voice was expressionless, but Betsy had the feeling that he was keeping something back and exerting fierce control over his emotions.

The media portrayed Carlos as a shallow playboy who preferred to party with his jet-set friends and surrounded himself with a bevy of beautiful women. But the man she had got to know during those few weeks when she'd worked as his housekeeper had been unexpectedly insightful. Carlos had even told her about the Segarra Foundation, a charity he had set up with the aim of giving children from deprived backgrounds access to all sports and in particular tennis.

Betsy had been charmed by him once before, and it would be easy to fall under his spell again, she thought as she sipped her coffee. But she was no longer a naïve young woman with a head full of dreams. Becoming a single mother had made her grow up fast.

'I can't marry you,' she said abruptly.

Her hand was unsteady when she placed her cup back on the saucer and the delicate china rattled.

'Why not?'

She glanced at him, surprised that he sounded calm rather than confrontational, which he had been up until now.

'Isn't it obvious?'

Carlos frowned. 'Is there a boyfriend on the scene?'

'No. Bringing up a child alone doesn't leave much time for dating,' Betsy told him drily.

Silently she acknowledged that she compared every man to Carlos, and she had never been as fiercely attracted to anyone else.

'Then what are your objections? Every child needs a mother and a father.' There was an odd note in Carlos's voice that made Betsy curious. 'It would be better for our son to grow up with both his parents.'

'Would it?' She sighed. 'We don't even like each other, so how could we create a happy family for Sebastian? What if it didn't work out and we divorced? I won't risk putting Sebastian through a vicious custody battle like my parents did to me.'

Carlos gave her an intent look. 'You said you were eight when your parents' marriage ended. It sounds like it was a difficult time.'

'It was. I loved my mum and dad equally, but their divorce was acrimonious and I was torn between them. My loyalties were divided. I lost who *I* was because I tried so hard to make each of them happy.'

Betsy hated talking about her childhood. Even before her parents had split up there had been arguments and sulking, tears and tantrums on both sides. She had felt as if she was walking a tightrope. One wrong step and everything would come crashing down.

'The truth is that I was just something else my parents fought over—like money and who got the dog,' she told Carlos. 'But as their fights got louder and more vicious, the quieter I became. Sometimes I even considered running away. I thought that if I wasn't around they would stop arguing.'

'*Dios*. You actually thought that?'

'After the divorce I lived with my mother and I hoped that things would settle down…' She hesitated, reluctant to reveal how dysfunctional her family had been. But she needed to make him understand why she was so against marriage. 'It all blew up when my dad kidnapped me.'

She could not bring herself to look at Carlos, but she sensed from his silence that she had shocked him.

He swore softly. 'No wonder you were terrified when you woke up and found Sebastian missing from his cot.'

Had there been sympathy in his voice? She felt the press of tears behind her eyelids and quickly brushed her hand over her eyes. 'I was scared you had taken my baby.'

Carlos exhaled slowly. 'Of course I don't want to separate you and Sebastian.' His tone hardened. 'But he is my son and I won't walk away from him. Marriage will allow us to both be part of his life.'

'The idea of getting married fills me with dread,' Betsy admitted in a low voice. 'My parents were feted as a golden couple on both sides of the Atlantic. The beautiful actress and the brilliant writer. My mother kept newspaper clippings of their fairy-tale wedding. She told me that she and my father had been madly in love. I have a few early memories of the three of us being a happy family. But when things started to go wrong I believed that their rows were my fault.'

She forced herself to meet Carlos's gaze.

'The point I'm trying to make is that my parents married because they were in love, but they ended up hating each other and their divorce destroyed my childhood. You and I barely know each other, and we are certainly not in love. If we married it would be a disaster—for us and more importantly for Sebastian.'

'I disagree,' he said coolly. 'Our marriage will work precisely because it *won't* be founded on a romantic ideal. Your parents fell out of love and you suffered as a consequence. What I am suggesting is an alliance built on the shared goal of giving our son the stable family life that you wish you'd had and I was lucky enough to experience until my mother died.'

Carlos's voice was still carefully controlled, but Betsy sensed pain behind his words.

'Sebastian deserves to grow up feeling secure and loved by *both* his parents,' he continued. 'It is our responsibility to put his needs first.'

Betsy tried not to let his words invade her heart. She needed to think calmly and rationally. But when he'd mentioned family she'd remembered how she had envied her schoolfriends, whose parents did not throw things at each other, or slash their partners' clothes with a pair of scissors, as her mother had once done to her father's suits.

'It wouldn't work,' she muttered.

'It will be up to us to *make* it work,' Carlos said implacably. 'What is the alternative? That we share custody of Sebastian but live separate lives and date other people? You're single now, but you might meet someone in the future. I'll admit that I hate the idea of another man being a stepfather to my son. And it could happen the other way around. How would you feel if I had a relationship with a woman who would be Sebastian's stepmother?'

Betsy had no intention of handing Sebastian over to

another woman. She did not have good memories of her first stepmother, who had been her father's second wife. Her relationship with Drake had been strained after he had been released from prison. Betsy hadn't wanted him to be sent to prison, even though she'd understood that he had committed a crime by abducting her. She had hoped for a reconciliation, but when she'd visited him in Canada she'd discovered that Drake had remarried. His new wife had made it plain that she resented having a prepubescent stepdaughter foisted on her.

'I'm sure we can work out a way that will allow us to co-parent Sebastian without having to get married,' she insisted.

Carlos's steely expression made her heart sink.

'You might be willing for him to be teased by his classmates for being a bastard when he's old enough to understand, but I am not,' he said curtly.

'No one cares about that sort of thing any more.'

'My son will bear *my* name.'

The quiet determination in Carlos's voice exacerbated Betsy's tension.

Her shoulders slumped. 'I wish you hadn't found out about Sebastian.' She had not meant to utter the words out loud, but they seemed to ricochet off the walls.

'I'm not simply going to disappear out of the picture because it suits you,' he said harshly.

'I didn't mean…' But it had been a terrible thing to say and she felt ashamed.

'I am a well-known figure and the paparazzi will

continue to be interested in you and Sebastian. How could you ensure his protection?'

'Protection from what?'

'It's not a secret that I became a multi-millionaire from my tennis career and sponsorship deals. My investment portfolio and my sports management agency are also highly lucrative. There are people who would try to snatch my son and demand a ransom for his safe return.'

Carlos frowned when Betsy gave a low cry of distress.

'I'm not trying to scare you. I'm simply stating facts. But you don't need to worry. I will never allow any harm to come to Sebastian or to you. My security team are ex-marines and my house in Toledo was once a fortress.'

She could feel her heart thudding painfully hard in her chest. Maybe Carlos hadn't set out to frighten her, but he'd succeeded. She would never put her baby in danger.

'Would you deny Sebastian everything that should be his by right of birth?' Carlos pressed her. 'My name, the privileges and the security I can give him? A family?'

Betsy stood up and walked over to the window. The room overlooked the hotel's driveway and she saw a group of photographers standing by the front gates with their cameras mounted on tripods. Everything had changed. She and Sebastian would never be able to go back to living in obscurity in a sleepy Dorset village. And Carlos had said he would not walk away from his son and she believed him.

She turned away from the window and watched him lift Sebastian out of the highchair. Their physical likeness was startling, and Betsy felt a tug on her heart as she saw in Carlos the man her son would one day become. The prospect of marrying Carlos was terrifying, but her conscience would not allow her to deny him a relationship with Sebastian.

'*If* we were to marry, you say it will be an alliance?' She felt her way cautiously along a path that her instincts were screaming at her not to take.

He nodded. 'I want us to have an equal partnership in which we will discuss everything concerning our son's upbringing.'

'What if we disagree about something?' She remembered how, as a child, she would lie in bed and pull the duvet over her head to try and block out the sound of her parents rowing.

'We'll find a solution, make compromises...but Sebastian's best interests will always be our objective.'

A marriage proposal where love wasn't mentioned might seem odd to most people, but Betsy felt reassured that Carlos wanted a partnership. And if deep in her heart she still yearned for romance, and the promise of everlasting love, she quashed the feeling. Although when Carlos set Sebastian down on the rug with his toys and walked towards her, she couldn't control her racing pulse.

He stopped in front of her and his eyes narrowed to

gleaming gold slits. Jaguar's eyes that gave no clue to his thoughts.

'What is your answer, Betsy? Are you going to marry me for the sake of our son?'

She had no choice. For Sebastian she would do anything, even marry the devil. Betsy tilted her chin and met Carlos's hard gaze. 'I'll marry you on one condition.'

His dark brows lifted. The unexpected gentleness in his face made her want to cry. She had assumed he would be triumphant in victory. Was she crazy to believe they could actually make this work?

'I want us both to sign a prenuptial agreement, setting out how we will share caring for Sebastian if we divorce. I'll marry you so that he is legitimate and he can take your name. But if we separate in the future I don't want him to be the subject of a custody battle or feel that he has to choose between us.'

Her voice thickened with tears. Memories of her childhood were intensely painful, but she was sure that neither of her parents had understood how lonely and scared she'd felt, caught in the midst of their hatred of each other.

'And we will never argue in front of him. Whatever happens between us, Sebastian will only know love.'

Carlos looked startled for a moment, before he nodded. 'I'll have my legal team work out the details. You will only sign the prenuptial agreement when you are happy with it.'

'Thank you.'

Some of Betsy's tension drained away. Their marriage would not be made in heaven, but in a lawyer's office. It was the best way to protect Sebastian.

She could only hope that her heart would survive unscathed with her decision to marry her baby's dangerously fascinating father.

CHAPTER FIVE

'IT DOESN'T LOOK much like a fortress,' Betsy commented as she followed Carlos into the modern open-plan living space of his penthouse apartment in a fashionable area of Madrid.

He saw her catch her bottom lip between her teeth as she glanced around at the décor, pale grey sofas and white rugs on black marble floors. Perhaps she was thinking that the tinted glass cabinets lining one wall would be a magnet for an inquisitive toddler.

'I was referring to my house in Toledo,' he explained. 'Fortaleza Aguila was originally a fortress when it was built in the sixteenth century. I keep this apartment for when I stay in Madrid. There are security cameras in the lobby, and no one can enter the building who shouldn't,' he assured her, aware that she was concerned for Sebastian's safety.

He watched his son, wriggling in Betsy's arms.

'Why don't you put him down? He must want to stretch his legs after being confined in his child seat in the plane and then the car from the airport.'

'I'm worried he'll put sticky fingers on the cushions or slip over on the hard floor and bang his head. It's not exactly a child-friendly environment.'

She shifted Sebastian to her other hip. Carlos had the feeling that she was holding on to the baby because she felt unsure of herself now that they were in Spain.

Before leaving England they'd gone back to Fraddlington. Photographers had been waiting outside the gates of the hotel and there had been more of them in front of Betsy's cottage. She had directed the driver down a narrow alleyway at the rear of the property and they'd entered the cottage through the back door, without the paparazzi seeing them. Betsy had run upstairs and reappeared a short while later carrying just one suitcase.

'I'll arrange for the rest of your things to be packed up and sent out to Spain,' he'd told her.

She'd looked surprised. 'I don't own anything else. All my belongings and Sebastian's are in this case. I rented the cottage fully furnished, and everything, even the cushions, belongs to the landlord.'

Now the suitcase that held Betsy's entire worldly possessions looked forlorn against the backdrop of his luxurious penthouse. Guilt swirled inside Carlos. He would have provided for her and Sebastian if she had turned to him for help. Instead she had made a meagre living, working behind the bar of the village pub.

While they had been at the cottage she had changed into a black skirt and white blouse. Both items looked cheaply made, and her low-heeled black shoes were scuffed. The outfit was only marginally smarter than the ripped jeans and old trainers she'd worn the previous day.

Carlos's mouth tightened as it occurred to him that the skirt and blouse were probably her smartest clothes, and that she probably wore them when she worked as a barmaid. But the badly fitting clothes did not detract from her beauty. He could not explain why the curve of her cheek and the slight pout of her lips made his mouth run dry.

She was a natural English rose, with porcelain skin and doe eyes that could darken with temper. But right now they were regarding him with a wariness that irritated him. Did she not realise that her life was going to improve vastly when she became his wife? He had plenty of money, several beautiful homes, and she would never have to work again. Many women would jump at the chance to marry him.

But Betsy had good reason to view marriage with trepidation, Carlos reminded himself. She had clearly been affected by her parents' behaviour. Some of the newspapers had already raked up old reports of her parents' public and very nasty divorce, and Betsy had been visibly upset when she'd seen them. Her vulnerability tugged on Carlos's emotions, even though only a day ago he would have sworn that was impossible.

His eyes were drawn to the swell of her breasts outlined beneath her thin cotton blouse and he acknowledged that he had thought about her more often than he'd liked in the past two years.

'Do you *have* to look at me as if I'm a dog's dinner?' she muttered. 'I realise that I'm not sophisticated and glamorous, like the women you are usually photographed with.'

'There will have to be some changes to your wardrobe,' Carlos told her bluntly. 'With that in mind, I have arranged for you to meet a stylist who will take you shopping this afternoon.' Before Betsy could argue, he continued, 'We have come to Madrid to attend a charity fundraising ball for the Segarra Foundation. The paparazzi will be out in full to take pictures of the celebrity guests, and I intend to make a press statement announcing our forthcoming marriage.'

She frowned. 'What about Sebastian? His bedtime is seven o'clock and I'd like to keep him to his routine. I'm guessing the party will finish much later.'

'We will leave him behind. Not on his own, obviously.' Carlos forestalled the objection he sensed Betsy was about to make. 'He will be with a nanny. Once we are married we'll attend many social functions together, and it will be necessary to employ nursery staff to look after our son.'

Betsy glared at him. 'I can't believe you've hired a nanny without discussing it with me first. You promised that our marriage would be a partnership and that we would jointly make decisions about Sebastian. Now you have steamrollered ahead without asking my opinion. That's not an alliance, that's bullying, and I won't stand for it.'

Her voice had risen during her angry tirade and Sebastian's little face crumpled as he gave a whimper.

Betsy made a choked sound. 'Now we're arguing in front of him. I must have been mad to agree to marry you.'

Her voice wobbled, and Carlos stiffened when he saw a tear slip down her cheek.

'I haven't hired anyone,' he assured her, feeling guilty that he was the cause of Betsy's distress—it was a reminder of why he never made attachments. He was no good at it, and he let people down. 'My sister owns the apartment next door to this one and she has offered to have Sebastian for the night. He can sleep in the nursery with her son, and Miguel's nanny will be on hand to help Graciela with both boys.'

He'd hoped that his explanation would be enough to halt Betsy's tears, but her shoulders shook harder. 'I'm sorry,' she said in a choked voice. 'I'm just so *scared* that once we're married you'll try to take Sebastian away from me.'

'I swear that I will never do that.' Carlos wondered with a flash of anger if her parents had any idea how their behaviour had affected their daughter. 'Betsy, let me hold Sebastian while you pull yourself together.' He held out his hands and after a moment's hesitation she allowed him to take the baby. 'We'll advertise for a nanny once we are in Toledo. We will interview the applicants together, but ultimately the decision of who we employ will be yours, okay?'

'O-okay.' She swallowed and gave him something

approaching a smile. 'Sebastian is my world and I love him more than anything.'

He lifted his hand and brushed away a tear from Betsy's cheek. Her skin felt like satin and her eyes were soft, her expression a little stunned. Carlos had the feeling she did not allow herself to cry very often. He had intended to comfort her, but he was conscious of the rapid thud of his pulse as he inhaled the lemony scent of her hair. Barely aware of what he was doing, he lowered his head towards her, drawn to the lush temptation of her mouth.

He was abruptly brought to his senses when Sebastian chose that moment to voice his frustration at being held and gave a loud yell. Carlos stepped back from Betsy at the same time as she jerked away from him. And as he watched a pink stain run under her skin he realised that she felt the simmering sexual awareness between them as fiercely as he did.

'Come and let me introduce you to my sister and her little boy,' he said, moving away from the tempting package of this woman he was determined to marry and just as determined to keep at arm's length. Betsy tested his self-control, but he would not allow her to break it. 'Graciela is keen to meet Sebastian.'

Betsy stared out of the car window at the blaze of streetlights and car headlamps that lit up Madrid's most famous street at night. Earlier in the day an elegant stylist called Sanchia had taken her shopping on Gran Via. Betsy had lost count of the number of exclusive boutiques and designer stores they had visited. The clothes she'd tried on had received a nod of approval or a shake of the head from Sanchia, and the purchased items had been paid for with Carlos's credit card.

'You are going to be my wife. Like it or not I am a well-known public figure, and I want our marriage to appear genuine. I won't have you dressing like a waitress in a downtown diner,' he'd told her brutally when she had protested about the shopping trip.

By then everything about her new life had felt surreal, and Betsy had simply accepted the stylist's advice on clothes, shoes and accessories. After the shopping there had been a visit to a beauty salon, where glorious-smelling products had been applied to her hair and her skin.

But she had barely glanced at her reflection to see the new and improved version of herself because she had been anxious to get back to Sebastian. Although she need not have worried about him. When she'd returned to Carlos's sister's child-friendly apartment, Sebastian had been in the nursery with his cousin Miguel. Carlos, Graciela and the nanny had been playing with both children.

Betsy had halted outside the room, overwhelmed by a mix of emotions as she heard Sebastian laughing and watched him clamber onto Carlos's knee. Her little boy looked so happy with his new family. And Carlos's sister had been so welcoming when they had been introduced. Graciela had tactfully not asked why Betsy had kept Sebastian a secret.

She pulled her mind back to the present. The car was crawling along in heavy traffic, but she did not mind if their arrival at the party was delayed. Carlos had warned her that there was likely to be a large media presence at the hotel where the event was being held. When Betsy had been a child, the paparazzi had been obsessed with her celebrity parents during their hostile divorce.

Memories of intrusive photographers and their camera flashbulbs going off, plus the knowledge that she would have to face the paparazzi tonight, when she and Carlos stepped out of the car, were partly to blame for her tension. But the main reason why her nerves felt strung out was sprawled next to her on the back seat of the limousine.

She glanced at Carlos's austere profile and butterflies leapt in her stomach when he turned his head towards her. He was so impossibly handsome. The perfect symmetry of his features, those gleaming golden eyes beneath heavy brows and that mouth all promised sensual heaven. And delivered. The memory of his kiss had stayed with her for two long years.

She caught her bottom lip between her teeth. Carlos's eyes narrowed and he lifted his hand and brushed his thumb lightly over the place where she had bitten.

'Are you still worrying about Sebastian? He was fast asleep when we left him at my sister's apartment, and even if he does wake up Graciela and the nanny will take good care of him.'

'I know he will be fine.'

She ran her tongue over her lip, where it tingled from Carlos's touch. His gaze sharpened on her face and Betsy saw a glint of gold beneath his thick lashes. Awareness of his male potency caused the tiny hairs on her body to stand on end.

'I'm sorry I was an idiot earlier today,' she mumbled, embarrassment flaring because she had broken down in front of him.

They had flown to Spain on Carlos's private jet. When Betsy had seen his luxurious penthouse apartment it had been another sign that he was hugely wealthy. But she had grown up with money—although the only winners in her parents' divorce had been the lawyers—and she knew that affluence did not guarantee happiness.

She looked down at the exquisite pear-shaped diamond ring that Carlos had slid onto her finger before they had left his penthouse. The streetlights shining through the window glinted on the diamond so that it sparkled with a fiery brilliance. But the ring, like the designer dress she was wearing, was only to convince the paparazzi that her romance with Carlos was genuine.

Her heart gave a jolt when he captured her hand and lifted it to his mouth. The brush of his lips across her fingers sent a shiver of sensation through her.

'We will both need a period of adjustment,' he murmured. 'I accept that the trauma you experienced as a child when your parents divorced amid such acrimony led to your decision not to tell me about Sebastian. But our marriage will be different. I will do everything possible to make it work.'

Carlos sounded sincere. Betsy tried to remind herself that he was only marrying her to claim his son, but she did want Sebastian to grow up with parents who did not despise each other.

'I will do my best to make our marriage work, too,' she promised.

Her eyes locked with his and she could not look away from him. The atmosphere inside the car was suddenly thick with sexual awareness. Hers. His.

The privacy screen was up, separating them from the driver. Betsy's stomach dipped when Carlos took hold of her chin. She watched his dark head descend and held her breath. Her pulse was thudding and she was transfixed by the feral gleam in his eyes. His gaze was on her lips and she moistened them with the tip of her tongue.

'Perhaps we should seal the deal with a kiss?'

His deep voice was like velvet caressing her skin. She had secretly longed for him to kiss her from the moment he'd stormed into her cottage, Betsy admitted to herself. Her common sense told her to resist her attraction to him. He had the power to hurt her—as he had done once before, and as her father had done when he had dropped out of her life. But her body refused to listen to her brain, and she felt her breasts tighten and her thighs soften. The truth was that she was desperately attracted to Carlos and her lips parted in invitation.

'I agree,' she whispered, casting caution aside.

Anticipation ran like quicksilver through her veins when he dipped his head lower and closed the tiny gap between them. He grazed his lips across hers and she felt him smile before he covered her mouth with his own and kissed her with bone-shaking sensuality.

She caught fire instantly, unable to resist his bold mastery as he coaxed her lips apart with the tip of his tongue and then plundered deep inside her mouth. He released her chin and slid his hand round to her nape. She tipped her head back, twisting in her seat so that she could press her body against him. His fingers tangled in her hair and he skimmed his other hand from her waist to the curve of her breast.

His kiss was even better than she remembered… even more potent than her dreams of being in his arms. The reality was heat and flame and she was powerless to resist his mastery.

'You look incredible,' Carlos whispered against her mouth. 'When I first saw you in that dress you took my breath away.'

Pleasure swept through her at this husky compliment. The dress that the stylist had picked out was a floor-length forget-me-knot-blue silk sheath overlaid with lace and embellished with tiny sparkling crystals. The plunging neckline was more daring than anything Betsy had ever worn before, and the side split in the skirt went up to her mid-thigh. Strappy silver stilettos and a silver clutch bag were the perfect accessories.

Her make-up had been kept discreet and the stylist had left her hair loose.

When she'd walked into the sitting room at the apartment the look of admiration on Carlos's face had for a moment helped to ease her nerves about making her first public appearance with him. He looked mouthwatering in a black dinner suit, white silk shirt and black bow tie. The formal clothes emphasised his athletic physique, and his thick, dark hair curled rebelliously over his collar.

Betsy had drawn a sharp breath when he'd pulled a velvet box out of the pocket of his tuxedo and opened it to reveal the diamond engagement ring. 'Is that really necessary?' she'd muttered.

The ring had made her situation real. She had agreed to marry a man who did not love her. But at least Carlos had not made false promises—unlike her father, who had used her as a pawn in his battle of one-upmanship with her mother. In truth, both her parents had put their own selfish aims above her happiness, Betsy thought ruefully.

Now Carlos deepened the kiss, and the firm pressure of his lips on hers decimated the last vestiges of her defences. The world ceased to exist and there was only him. His arms felt like iron bands around her and his evocative scent—spicy cologne mingled with male pheromones—filled her senses. It had been the same two years ago. One kiss and she had been lost to the intoxicating pleasure that he'd wrought with his mouth and hands.

Right now one of his hands was on her back, tracing along her spine, and the other was splayed over her breast. His thumb stroked her peaked nipple through her dress, sending shockwaves of sensation through her. Desire pooled low in her pelvis and she curled her arms around his neck, so that her breasts were pressed hard against his chest. She could feel the beat of his heart echo the erratic thud of her own.

Outside the window there was a bright flash, then another, and another. Betsy blinked, suddenly aware that the car was no longer moving. Carlos lifted his mouth from hers and growled something in Spanish as he moved along the seat away from her.

Still dazed from their passion, she gave a soft moan of protest which turned into a choked sound of dismay as her brain clicked into gear and she realised they had arrived at the hotel. The blinding flashes had been from the paparazzi's cameras.

Carlos raked his fingers through his hair, and Betsy fancied that his hand was a little unsteady. But when he spoke his voice held its usual blend of cynicism and faint amusement, as if he took nothing in life too seriously. 'Are you ready for showtime?'

The door was opened by the chauffeur and Carlos climbed out of the car and offered his hand to help Betsy step onto the pavement. She was blinded by bright white light and heard the popping sound of more flashbulbs exploding. The press pack surged forward and she was glad of Carlos's solid presence beside her as he slid his arm around her waist. She was still stunned by that passionate kiss in the back of the car, but she told herself that her legs felt wobbly because she was unused to walking in high heels.

'Carlos—is it true that you and Miss Miller have a child?' a photographer called out.

'Why was your baby kept a secret?' someone else shouted.

'You are on record saying that you never wanted children, Carlos. Do you regret the birth of your son?'

Betsy felt Carlos tense as he led her up the steps of the hotel, but when he turned to face the baying press his bland expression revealed nothing of his thoughts.

'It is absolutely true that Miss Miller is the mother of my son,' he said calmly. 'And, far from regretting Sebastian's birth, I am delighted to be a father. Betsy and I had hoped to keep our son out of the spotlight, but now I am very happy to reveal that we intend to marry as soon as possible.'

A babble of voices rose from the crowd of paparazzi.

A photographer pushed closer to Betsy. 'Miss Miller, your high-profile parents went through a notoriously acrimonious divorce and fought for custody of you when you were a child. Your father even kidnapped you at one point. Has that had an effect on how you view marriage?'

She stiffened. The question was intrusive, and it brought back memories she wished she could forget. But she would deal with her demons in private—not in the pages of the tabloids. Ignoring a strong urge to run into the hotel, away from the camera lenses, she forced a smile for the paparazzi.

'My view of marriage is that it is a wonderful institution and I am looking forward to becoming Carlos's wife.' She held out her left hand to show off the engagement ring. 'Diamonds really are a girl's best friend,' she quipped. 'I'm extremely happy.'

To her relief, Carlos ignored further questions from the press and escorted her inside the hotel. As they walked through the opulent foyer Betsy's stiletto heels clicked on the marble floor.

Carlos glanced at her. 'You handled that well.'

The admiration in his voice made her foolish heart leap. She halted and turned to face him.

'Some people sympathised with my father when he kept me hidden in Canada. He was seen as a champion of the rights of fathers. He said he kidnapped me because he loved me, and I felt terrible when he was sent to prison. When he was released I hoped I could rebuild my relationship with him. But I was a teenager by then, and Drake lost interest in me when he realised that he couldn't use me as a way to hurt my mother any more.'

She sighed.

'I'm telling you this because I don't want you to make a public show of claiming your son only to become bored with fatherhood when Sebastian reaches the tantrums stage or when he is no longer a cute toddler.'

An indefinable expression flickered in Carlos's eyes. 'My commitment to my son will be total and for ever.'

She nodded, feeling reassured.

Ahead of them, the double doors leading to the ballroom stood open and guests were already filling the room.

'I'd like to use the bathroom.' She needed a few moments to steel her nerves before she put on a show as Carlos's fiancée.

Thankfully the cloakroom was empty, and there was no one to hear Betsy's groan of dismay when she saw her reflection in the mirror. Her hair was mussed and the neckline of her dress was askew. She ran her finger over lips that were still puffy from Carlos's kisses.

Her stomach swooped as she wondered if he had kissed her deliberately, knowing that the photographers would snap pictures of her looking suitably lovestruck. He had warned her that the paparazzi would be waiting for them, but she had forgotten, or simply not cared, because when Carlos had put his mouth on hers she had been instantly lost in the beauty of his kiss.

After reapplying a pale pink gloss to her lips, and taking several deep breaths, she went to find him.

The hotel foyer was crowded now, as more guests arrived. Carlos was standing by the entrance to the ballroom and, Betsy noticed that all the beautiful women gravitated towards him like bees drawn to honey. He looked over in her direction and the lazy smile on his face turned into something far more predatory. The heat of his gaze burned through her and she felt an ache in her womb.

He was the father of her child, and soon she would be his wife, but what did Carlos expect from their marriage—from her? She bit her lip. They'd had sex once, and the next morning he'd left. Those facts were unarguable. If she hadn't had Sebastian she would not be wearing Carlos's ring now. But he had said he wanted their marriage to work—did that mean he wanted to have sex with her?

Shockingly explicit memories flooded her mind of his powerful body looming above her, his thick erection pushing deeper and deeper inside her. Between her legs she felt the sticky heat of desire...

He could not possibly know what she was thinking, she assured herself as she walked towards him. But the golden gleam in his eyes sent her pulse racing and she could not look away from him.

His dark brows quirked. 'Ready?'

Betsy felt a betraying blush spread across her face. She might as well have 'ready for sex' tattooed on her forehead, she thought ruefully. Carlos made her forget her natural caution and behave in a way she had never done with any other man.

But two years ago she had given him her virginity and, although she hadn't expected the night they had spent together to lead to everlasting love, she had felt such a fool when he'd gone back to Spain without a word. She would enter this marriage with no expectations, she vowed silently, and she would guard her heart against Carlos.

Giving him a cool smile, she slipped her hand through the arm that he held out to her and walked beside him into the ballroom.

CHAPTER SIX

THE CHARITY BALL was a spectacular event that would be talked about for weeks afterwards. Carlos had expected nothing less. He employed the best party planners and had funded the event personally. The food was sublime, the champagne flowed, the guests were clearly enjoying themselves—and, most importantly, a substantial amount of money was being raised for the Segarra Foundation.

Since he'd retired from playing tennis competitively, Carlos's passion had been his charity, which aimed to enable kids from deprived backgrounds to access sports which were too often elitist. As a child he had been lucky, because his mother had once been a professional tennis player and had not only encouraged his talent but managed to secure funding for his training. The foundation was his way of putting something back into the world of sport that had made him a household name and a multi-millionaire.

The evening was drawing to an end and he should be feeling satisfied. But Carlos grimaced as he acknowledged that *satisfied* was the opposite of how he felt.

Frustration surged through him as he moved around the dance floor with Betsy in his arms. Holding her close like this was pure torture. He was fiercely aware of her soft breasts pressed against his chest, and when the side split in her ballgown parted and he felt the brush of a stocking-clad leg against his thigh, it took all his willpower not to haul her closer still. But if he did she would be bound to realise that he was aroused.

It infuriated him that she made him feel dangerously out of control when no other woman had ever done more than spark his temporary interest. He shouldn't have kissed her in the car. That was when everything had gone wrong. He'd tasted her sweet breath in his mouth and a madness had come over him.

Carlos tried to blame his obsession with Betsy on his libido, which had inconveniently reawakened after the longest period of celibacy he'd had since his first sexual experience when he was sixteen.

He looked down at the top of Betsy's head as she rested it on his chest. The silky caramel curls invited him to spear his fingers in her hair and angle her head so that he could taste her again and plunder the moist lips that she'd parted beneath his during those stolen moments in the back of the limousine.

Maybe she'd sensed his scrutiny, for she looked up at him and he saw her brown eyes darken as the pupils dilated. He could not fault her performance. Why, she had almost convinced *him*, along with the guests and invited members of the press, that she was his adoring fiancée.

For a moment he imagined that this was real. That they were two people who had connected on a fundamental level and were eagerly anticipating spending the rest of their lives together...

Dios. He cursed silently as he reminded himself that the only reason he was marrying Betsy was so that he could be a full-time father to his son.

There was a lull in the music and Betsy gave him a rueful smile as she pulled out of his arms, leaving him with a sense of regret that added to his fury with himself.

'I'll have to sit this one out,' she said. 'My feet are killing me.'

'The ball is due to finish soon—I was about to suggest that we should leave.'

He was aware that he sounded curt, and caught the look of surprise she darted at him, but he felt marginally more in control now that her delectable body wasn't pressed up against him.

He took out his phone and instructed his driver to bring the car to the front of the hotel.

Five minutes later Betsy blew out a breath as she leaned against the plush leather seat in the back of the car. 'Sorry, but I can't wear my shoes for a second longer.'

'Put your seat belt back on,' Carlos ordered as she released the belt and leaned down to fiddle with her shoes.

'I will in a minute...'

He swore as the car turned a sharp corner and she

was flung against him. The sensation of her voluptuous curves pressed against him rattled his hard-won composure and, after securing the seat belt around her once more, he lifted her legs across his lap. His fingers brushed across her slender ankles as he unfastened the tiny buckles on her shoes.

Betsy gave a deep sigh as she kicked off her shoes and wriggled her toes. '*Oh*…that's better.'

Her smile lit up her lovely face and Carlos's heart kicked in his chest.

'The ball seemed to go well. Not that I have much experience of grand parties. The most popular social event at the pub was darts night, when Fraddlington's team played against teams from other villages.'

'Why did you move to Dorset?' he asked, needing to distract his mind from her slender legs lying across his lap. The split in her skirt had parted to reveal a toned thigh…

'My aunt died and the house in London was sold. Sarah is an old school friend and she offered me a job at the pub that she and Mike had bought in Fraddlington. The landlord of the cottage I rented is a friend of Mike's.'

'What about your parents? Didn't they help you after Sebastian was born?'

'Mum came to visit, but she only stayed for a week. She has lived in LA for a few years now, and she has a new husband. As for my dad…' A look of sadness crossed Betsy's face. 'We keep in contact sporadically, but he's married again too—to his third wife. After he kidnapped me our relationship was never as close as it had been before,' she said flatly.

Carlos turned his gaze away from her and stared out of the window. Betsy's vulnerability tugged on something inside him and he felt surprisingly protective of her. Neither of her parents had been good role models and they had never prioritised their daughter's need for security. But, in contrast, Betsy was a devoted mother to Sebastian and, despite her reservations, she had accepted that marriage to him would allow the little boy to grow up in a safe family environment.

The car pulled into the underground car park and Betsy carried her shoes to the lift, which whisked them up to the top floor of the apartment block. The mirrored walls inside the lift gave Carlos a view of her gorgeous figure from every angle.

She was a pocket Venus, standing there in her stockinged feet, with her long skirt gathered in one hand and her shoes dangling by their straps from the other. He fancied that her mouth was still slightly swollen from where he'd kissed her earlier, and the memory of her lips parting beneath his made his body clench hard.

He ushered her into the penthouse, which had been designed as his bachelor pad but hadn't seen a lot of action in the past two years. In fact he couldn't remember the last time he'd invited a woman back for the night.

Carlos had put his lack of interest in sex down to his change of lifestyle after he'd retired from playing tennis professionally. Achieving the pinnacle of his ambition by winning the tournament in London had left him feeling unsettled and directionless. Grief for his mother, which he'd managed to supress for nearly two decades, had suddenly hit him hard, and guilt had consumed him.

It still did.

Betsy had headed down the corridor towards the guest bedroom. Carlos told himself he was relieved that there would be no further chance for her to flirt with him tonight. Because that was what she'd been doing at the ball—with a shy hesitancy that had affected him much more than if she'd come on to him with the boldness of a *femme fatale*.

As he strode across the lounge he pulled off his bow tie and unfastened the top buttons on his shirt. He extracted a bottle of single malt Scotch from the drinks cabinet, poured a measure into a glass—and stiffened when he sensed that he wasn't alone.

Betsy—minus shoes and evening purse—stood in the doorway.

'I thought you had gone to bed.' Good manners compelled him to ask, 'Is there anything I can get you?'

'I wouldn't mind a nightcap.'

Her husky voice tugged low in his gut. Carlos poured whisky into a second glass and reminded himself that women had thrown themselves at him since he was sixteen. He could handle this unremarkable, unsophisticated woman. No problem.

He carried their drinks over to the coffee table and lowered himself down onto the sofa. An alarm bell rang in his head when Betsy sat next to him. She leaned forward to pick up her glass, and lust speared him in the groin as his gaze was drawn to the front of her dress and the creamy upper slopes of her breasts.

She took a sip of her drink, and Carlos had an idea that she needed the kick of alcohol.

'I would like to clarify a point about our marriage,' she murmured, fixing her big brown eyes on his face.

'Go on.' His gaze narrowed on the pink flush that spread across her cheeks.

'I'm not sure what you will want in…in the bedroom. What I mean is…will we share a bed?'

She caught her lower lip between her teeth, and it was all Carlos could do to restrain himself from demonstrating exactly what he wanted. Her—naked and willing beneath him.

'You say that your commitment to Sebastian will be total, but what about your commitment to our marriage?' Betsy was becoming visibly more embarrassed, but she ploughed on. 'What I'm asking is, will you want me to be a proper wife, or do you intend to keep a mistress discreetly in the background?'

Carlos stretched out his long legs and hooked one ankle over the other. He took a swig of whisky before he answered. 'Would you object if I kept a mistress?' he asked.

'Would it matter if I objected?' She put her head on one side and studied him. 'You've made it clear that you're calling all the shots.'

That vulnerability was there again in her voice. Carlos told himself that if he was a better man her words might have stirred his conscience. But his gaze was drawn to the rise and fall of Betsy's breasts as she took a deep breath.

'I'm simply trying to determine if you will…seek gratification outside of our marriage,' she murmured. 'And, if so, then it will only be fair for me to enjoy the same freedom.'

Over his dead body, Carlos thought violently.

He knew he should be appalled by the jealousy that surged like molten lava through his veins at the idea of Betsy warming another man's bed. Possessiveness was not one of his faults, though God knew he had enough of them. But the proprietorial feeling remained.

'The thing is…' she said softly.

She put her glass on the table and inched along the sofa towards him. Carlos breathed in her perfume, sweetly floral with underlying notes of something musky and deeply sensual that called to the wolf in him.

'You kissed me and…well…'

Her blush spread down her throat and over the slopes of her breasts, giving them the appearance of rose-flushed peaches, plump and firm and infinitely inviting. Carlos could see the outline of her nipples through her dress, and recalled how they had bloomed beneath his touch when he'd cupped her breasts in his hands during those crazy moments in the back of the car.

'Well… I liked it when you kissed me…'

Her honesty felt like a knife in his ribs.

'And I got the impression that you are still attracted

to me. So I'm wondering what you want from our relationship when we marry…or…or even before the wedding.'

So much for his belief that he could handle her! Carlos mocked himself. She tied him in knots, and he resented it.

He stood up abruptly and paced across the room to stand by the window. Before him Madrid was a mass of glittering lights against the backdrop of an inky sky. He was sorely tempted to respond to Betsy's sweetly clumsy invitation by carrying her into the bedroom so that he could make love to her. It was what they both wanted.

But something in her eyes told him that she might hope for more than sex—if not immediately then in the future, after they were married. And she would be disappointed. Because he had no intention of falling in love with her. Love meant responsibility, commitment and pain. Carlos had spent the past twenty years avoiding all three, and he was determined to maintain the status quo.

'I will commit to our marriage and I will expect you to do the same,' he growled as he swung round to face her. 'As you pointed out, there is an attraction between us. I foresee that in the future we will have a sexual relationship—especially when you are my wife and we sleep in the same bedroom at my house in Toledo.'

Betsy frowned. 'You want us to share a room?'

'It's customary for married couples to do so,' he said drily. 'But I advise you not to get carried away, nor to forget that we are marrying for the sake of our son. This is not a fairy-tale romance.'

'I'm well aware that you are not Prince Charming,' Betsy snapped.

Carlos watched her turn pale and then flush scarlet once more. Her eyes had darkened with anger, or maybe it was hurt. His conscience pricked again, but he reminded himself that her antipathy was safer than her sweetly clumsy attempt to seduce him.

'You are so *unbelievably* arrogant.'

She jumped to her feet and marched across the room to stand in front of him. But he noticed that she kept a distance between them, and he was glad. The temptation to reach out and pull her into his arms, lose whatever remained of his sanity in her glorious curves, still beat hard in him.

'Two years ago you must have realised I was a virgin, but you went back to Spain without a word—without checking if I was okay.'

'Was it really your first time?' he asked gruffly.

He had not forgotten anything about that night. Her eagerness to make love had delighted him. He had been surprised that she'd seemed to lack experience, but he'd been so hungry for her that he hadn't cared when her hands had fumbled with the zip on his trousers, or when she'd curled her fingers around his erection and squeezed him so enthusiastically that he'd almost come there and then.

'Yes. I wouldn't lie about it.'

His gaze narrowed on her flushed face. 'Why me?

You must have had boyfriends before we met—yet you were still a virgin. In your note you said you had slept with me because I was famous. Was that true?'

She dropped her gaze and suddenly seemed to be fascinated with the rug beneath her feet. 'I felt like an idiot when I overheard you telling that journalist that I was a casual fling. The truth is I had sex with you because I fancied you more than any of the guys I dated at university. Although, to be honest, there weren't many. My parents' volatile relationship wasn't a great advertisement for love,' she said wryly. 'But I liked you, and I thought you liked me. I should have known that the sexiest man in Spain would only want a one-night stand with someone like me.'

He frowned. 'Someone like you?'

'Ordinary. You only noticed me because we'd shared a house and I'd cooked your meals. I've seen photos in magazines of the women you date. They're always beautiful and glamorous.'

And shallow, Carlos thought. He could not remember individual faces, let alone the names of his past lovers. Only Betsy Miller had lodged like a burr beneath his skin.

'You shouldn't believe everything you read in the gossip columns,' he said drily. 'For what it's worth, I believe in being truthful as much as you. And I told you, I *did* try to contact you a few weeks after I'd left your aunt's house.'

A tiny frown appeared between her brows. 'I moved from there soon after you had left. My aunt died unexpectedly and her son Lee was her sole heir. He told me that I had to leave because he wanted to sell the house. A removals firm came and took all the furniture and Aunt Alice's personal belongings to a storage unit. I had just found out that I was pregnant, and I asked Lee if I could stay at the house while I looked for somewhere else to live, but he insisted that I had no legal right to stay there and I had to leave immediately.'

'*Dios!*' Carlos was enraged. 'What kind of man would make a pregnant young woman homeless?'

But he was hardly in a position to judge, he thought grimly. He should have stayed and spoken to Betsy the morning after he'd slept with her. It was true that he'd rushed back to Spain to be with his sister, but he'd received the call from Graciela saying that her baby needed heart surgery when he'd already been in the car on his way to the airport.

If he was honest, he'd felt shaken by his spectacular loss of control with Betsy. That first time with her had been the most satisfying sexual experience he'd ever had. Almost immediately after they'd both climaxed, while he was still inside her, he'd felt himself harden again. He'd quickly changed the condom, but his carelessness was a possible explanation for how she'd fallen pregnant, Carlos realised.

He took a gulp of whisky. 'Even then, when you had nowhere to live and had just found out that you were pregnant with my baby, you didn't ask for my help. Did you believe that I was a man like your aunt's son and I would turn my back on you?'

She had not given him a chance to accept responsibility for his child—perhaps because she had believed in his playboy reputation and the scurrilous gossip written about him to feed a celebrity-obsessed audience.

Guilt ripped through him and he turned away from her. From now on he would give Betsy and their son his protection, Carlos vowed to himself. But that was all he could give her. He had locked his emotions away twenty years ago, when his mother had died and he'd blamed himself.

'Earlier this evening we both agreed to do everything possible to make this a successful marriage,' Betsy said quietly. 'Why did you kiss me?'

Carlos remained where he stood in front of the window and narrowed his eyes until the bright city lights splintered. 'I am a red-blooded male and you made it clear that you wanted to be kissed.'

Behind him he heard her draw a sharp breath. He watched her reflection in the window as she spun round and marched out of the room.

He continued to stand there for a long time afterwards, alone with his demons. Spain's most famous sportsman, an international celebrity, and he was the loneliest man in the world.

CHAPTER SEVEN

BETSY'S PHONE PINGED and her stomach swooped when she saw Carlos's name flash on the screen. It was three weeks since she had woken in the guest bedroom at his penthouse the morning after the charity ball. As soon as she'd opened her eyes she had cringed with embarrassment as she'd recalled how she had propositioned him. She might not have actually *asked* him to have sex with her, but she had dropped unsubtle hints and he had rejected her.

She couldn't understand why she had behaved so out of character. Usually she was so reticent about her feelings.

She had no intention of falling in love with him, Betsy assured herself, but when Carlos had kissed her in the car they had both gone up in flames. His mouth had been hot and demanding as he'd deepened the kiss so that it had become something *more*—something wilder and needier. She had felt the proof of his desire when she'd laid her hand on his chest and felt the thunderous beat of his heart. And when they had danced together at the ball her wayward body had melted against him and she'd been very aware of the hard ridge of his arousal beneath his trousers.

Two years ago passion had exploded between them with their first kiss, and the same thing had happened here in Madrid.

Betsy knew she hadn't imagined the feral gleam in Carlos's eyes. She had thought of nothing else for the past three weeks. But that morning she had been in an agony of embarrassment, and he'd been coolly aloof in the car when he'd driven them to Toledo, an hour south of the capital.

She had opted to sit in the back with Sebastian, who had been strapped into his baby seat.

Carlos's house stood on a hill overlooking the historical city which had been immortalised by Spain's most famous artist El Greco in his painting *View of Toledo*. And Betsy had been pleasantly surprised to find that although Fortaleza Aguila still bore the evidence that it had once been a fortress, it was now an attractive house built of mellow brick, with terracotta roof tiles which had faded to a dusky pink in the blazing summer sun.

'The English translation of the house's name is Eagle Fortress,' Carlos had told her, when she'd forgotten her awkwardness with him for a few moments and looked with interest at the home that would now be hers and Sebastian's too.

She had felt daunted by all the huge changes to her life—not least when Carlos had lifted Sebastian out of the car and carried him into the house, leaving her to follow him.

The décor was traditionally Spanish, with dark wood panelling, ornate wall tiles and stone floors that were worn smooth with age. Betsy had recognised several original pieces of art that must be worth a fortune. It was all very beautiful, and something of a surprise after the modern penthouse in Madrid, but she felt like a visitor to a stately mansion.

'I arranged for an interior designer to create a nursery for Sebastian, and the decorators have just finished,' Carlos had told her as he'd opened a door on the second floor and ushered her into a large, sun-filled room.

Painted in tones of pale blue, white and yellow, and filled with toys, with a magnificent wooden cot in the centre, it was the kind of nursery Betsy had imagined planning for Sebastian if she won the Lottery. Carlos had set Sebastian on his feet and he'd toddled across the floor towards another oversized fluffy toy rabbit.

'Bun,' he'd said happily, before going off to investigate a pile of colourful plastic bricks.

The nursery was at least four times the size of the box room at the cottage, where Sebastian had slept in a travel cot that had belonged to the landlord. Guilt had been like a lead weight in the pit of Betsy's stomach as she'd acknowledged that Carlos could provide Sebastian with the kind of affluent lifestyle that would have been impossible for her to do on her income from her bar job and her paintings.

'This is your room,' Carlos had told her, and he'd opened a door from the nursery into an adjoining bedroom.

Betsy hadn't known whether she felt relieved or disappointed that he clearly did not expect her to sleep in his room straight away.

She pulled her mind back to the present and added a few more brushstrokes of white paint around the muzzle on the portrait she was working on. This commission had been a welcome surprise. The owners of the Labrador she'd painted while she had been at the cottage had been delighted with the portrait, which she'd had taken to the framers just before she'd left Fraddlington with Carlos. They had recommended her to a friend of theirs, and her new client had emailed photos of his beautiful chocolate and white Springer Spaniel.

It felt good to be painting again. Betsy had brought her brushes from England, but she'd needed more paints and canvases, and had been pleased when she'd discovered there was an art supplies shop in Toledo. She did not have a driving licence, but Carlos had arranged for his driver to take her into the city whenever she wanted to go.

When she'd walked into the art shop for the first time she'd carried her Spanish phrasebook, but to her relief the young assistant there spoke fluent English, albeit with a distinctive Brummie accent.

Hector's arms were covered in artistic tattoos and he had long black hair and wore big silver earrings. He looked like one of the art students Betsy had known at university.

'My dad is Spanish and I lived in Spain until I was twelve, when my parents split up and I moved to Birmingham with my mum,' he'd explained.

Hector was friendly—and *ordinary*, compared to Carlos's friends, who were all wealthy high-fliers. Betsy had become a regular visitor to his art shop, and found Hector was the only person she could really talk to. There was Carlos, of course, but her awareness of him was stronger than ever. And her fear of making a fool of herself, like she'd done at the penthouse, meant that she avoided being alone with him whenever possible.

With a faint sigh, she put down her brush and wiped her hands on a rag before she picked up her phone to read Carlos's message.

Come to my study so that we can discuss the wedding.

She grimaced as she pictured his autocratic features and rashly messaged back.

Yes, sir!

Her old jeans were covered in paint stains. She quickly changed out of them and put on one of her new dresses—a pale lemon silk wrap style, with a pretty floral pattern. She pulled the elastic tie from her hair and slicked pink gloss over her lips, assuring herself that as Carlos's future wife she couldn't run around the house in her old jeans. She hadn't changed her clothes in the hope of pleasing him, she told her reflection.

She went through the door from her bedroom that led directly into the nursery. Sebastian had been having his morning nap while she painted, but when she stepped into the room he wasn't in his cot. The nanny was there, folding some of Sebastian's new clothes.

Betsy had liked Ginette the moment she'd met her. English by birth, she had moved to Spain some twenty years ago, when she'd married her Spanish husband, and she spoke both languages fluently.

'My husband and I were not blessed with children of our own,' Ginette had explained at her interview. 'But I have loved looking after the children of the families I worked for. Now that Ernesto has passed away, I'm looking for a live-in position.'

Ginette smiled now, when she saw Betsy. 'Sebastian woke up about ten minutes ago, and Carlos took him downstairs.'

'We will need a period of adjustment.'

Carlos's words came back to Betsy and she acknowledged the truth of them. She had been her son's sole carer since he was born, and she was finding it hard to share the responsibility for him.

Her heart gave a jolt when she walked down the stairs and watched Sebastian toddling across the stone-flagged entrance hall, chasing after a plastic football. Carlos was crouched at one end of the hall and holding his arms out to his son.

'*Bueno, chico!* Kick the ball, *conejito.*'

'I think he might be a bit young to learn how to play football,' Betsy said drily, trying to hide her emotional response to seeing Sebastian so happy with his father. She wanted to scoop her baby into her arms and breathe in the delicious scent of him, but it was Carlos's arms that Sebastian ran to. She couldn't pretend to herself that it didn't hurt. 'You're already speaking to him in Spanish? Don't you think it will be confusing for him? He doesn't know many English words yet.'

Carlos lifted Sebastian up and strolled over to her. 'We agreed to bring him up to be bilingual,' he reminded her. 'And the best way for him to learn will be for him to hear words in both languages.'

That was fine for Carlos, who spoke English as fluently as his native tongue. But she would have to learn to speak Spanish quickly, otherwise she would be excluded from the relationship that Carlos and Sebastian would share when they talked in Spanish.

Maybe Carlos *wanted* to exclude her, Betsy brooded.

His gaze narrowed on her face. 'Is something the matter?'

She wasn't going to admit how vulnerable she felt. 'I was just thinking that Sebastian has adapted well to living here.'

'This is his home—and yours. Are you not adapting well, *querida*?'

Betsy made a mental note to ask Ginette what *querida* meant. She bit her lip. 'It's just very different to the life I had in England.'

Carlos stretched out his hand and ran his thumb lightly across her lower lip, where she had bitten the skin. 'I realise that everything here is new for you, and I appreciate it that you have allowed me to bring Sebastian to Spain.'

The warmth in his sherry-gold eyes curled around Betsy's heart. She refrained from pointing out that he hadn't given her much choice about where Sebastian would grow up. Since they had arrived in Toledo she'd gained a better understanding of how important it was to Carlos that Sebastian should bear his name. He was proud of his Spanish heritage and proud of his son. She saw it in the way his features softened every time he looked at the toddler who bore such a striking resemblance to him.

Betsy did not doubt that Carlos loved Sebastian, and that was why she had agreed to marry him. But she still felt like a fish out of water in this new country where the language, culture and customs were so different from the way of life she was used to in England.

Carlos seemed to have an uncanny knack of being able to read her thoughts. 'You will feel more settled once you are my wife,' he said softly.

The golden glint in his eyes caused Betsy's heart to miss a beat, and she could not look away from him. Time seemed to slow, and the air quivered with their mutual awareness. But then he blinked, and the connection she had sensed between them vanished. He looked across the hall and, following his gaze, she saw Ginette walking towards them.

'I thought I'd put Sebastian in his pushchair and take him for a walk in the garden,' Ginette said as she took him from Carlos.

'He will need to wear sunscreen.' Betsy was immediately a mother hen, determined to protect her chick. The temperature in Toledo in July was much hotter than the soggy English summer they had left behind. 'And don't forget to put the parasol up.'

'Ginette is highly experienced in childcare and has excellent references,' Carlos murmured when the nanny had carried Sebastian away.

'I know. But it's a mother's instinct to take care of her child and put his welfare above everything else.'

An odd expression flickered on his face, but it was gone before Betsy could decipher it. He said no more as he opened the door to his study and ushered her into the room.

'Have you heard from your parents?' he asked, waving her to a chair before he walked around the desk and sat down.

'I invited both of them to the wedding, as you suggested. But I warned you it would be pointless. My mother says she won't attend if my father brings "the trollop he is married to now", and Drake refuses to come without his third wife.' She shrugged. 'It was the same when I invited my parents to my graduation ceremony after university. They wanted me to choose between them, which I refused to do. The result was that neither of them came. I can't please one without upsetting the other.'

It was her childhood all over again, Betsy thought dismally. Her parents were the reason why she had never wanted to marry. Her chest felt tight with panic at the idea of being trapped in an unhappy relationship.

'I'm not sure I can do this,' she told Carlos.

Once again he seemed to read her mind. 'Our marriage won't be like theirs.'

'How do you know? We might fight all the time, and Sebastian will be caught in the middle like I was when I was a child.'

'The whole reason we are marrying is to give him a family. We are putting our child's needs first—which, from the sound of it, your parents failed to do with you.'

Carlos stood up and walked around to where she was sitting. He leaned his hip against the desk, much too close for Betsy's comfort. His fitted black trousers emphasised his rangy frame, and his white shirt was open at the throat, giving her a glimpse of his tanned skin and black chest hair.

She sighed. If only he wasn't so beautiful. She wished she could control her body's unbidden response to his potent masculinity, but when she lifted her hand to her throat she could feel the betraying thud of her pulse.

'You said that you would put Sebastian's welfare above everything else,' Carlos reminded her. 'And that means marrying me.'

She nodded. Sebastian adored his *papà*, and it had become increasingly clear to her that she did not have the right to separate her son from his father, nor deny Sebastian his Spanish heritage.

'I do want him to be legitimate. I expect all brides have pre-wedding jitters,' she forced herself to say lightly.

Carlos released his breath slowly. 'Is it important to you that your parents attend the wedding?'

'I *would* like my father to give me away, and my mother to be at the church wearing an outrageous mother-of-the-bride hat.' Betsy's sigh was unconsciously wistful. 'But it will be easier if they're not there. At least Sarah and Mike are coming, and a few of my friends from university. Although my side of the church is going to look very empty when the three hundred guests you have invited fill the pews on the other side.'

She dropped her gaze from Carlos's and stared at the huge diamond sparkling like a teardrop on her finger.

'Why do we have to have such a big wedding in full view of the media? It's going to be a circus, and I'll be the clown,' she muttered.

Carlos frowned. 'Would you prefer it if we sneaked off to the local town hall and married in secret? There have been too many secrets,' he said grimly. 'My tennis career gave me international fame, and being a public figure allows me to promote the Segarra Foundation. It is important to me that in the eyes of the world I am seen to be doing the right thing by marrying the mother of my son. When Sebastian is old enough to understand he will know that I wanted him, and that I do not regret his birth as some of the tabloids have speculated.'

His fiercely spoken words dispelled the last of

Betsy's doubts. Her conscience pricked. She should tell him how much she regretted the way she'd handled the situation two years ago, when she'd discovered that she was pregnant. For the first time she really tried to imagine how he must have felt when he read in a newspaper that he was a father, and his sense of betrayal when the paternity test had proved that Sebastian was his son.

'Fine—we'll do the wedding your way,' she mumbled.

'I understand that the stylist has helped you choose a bridal gown?'

'Yes. I'm having a fitting later today.'

She felt a thrill of guilty pleasure as she pictured the dress. The stylist had picked out an elegant, understated gown in ivory silk, but Betsy had been drawn to a confection of pure white tulle. Reasoning that she was only going to get married once—unlike her parents, who had so far clocked up five weddings between them—she had decided she wanted her dress to be a fairy tale even if her marriage was not.

With a sweetheart neckline, exquisite lace detail on the bodice and a sweeping train, the wedding dress was worthy of a princess. Betsy hoped it would disguise the fact that she was an ordinary girl who had captured the attention but not the heart of the man dubbed Spain's sexiest sporting legend.

'My father wants to meet his grandson,' Carlos told her. 'He was discharged from hospital yesterday, and has been resting this morning, but I've had a message from his nurse to say that he is awake now.'

Betsy knew that Roderigo Segarra lived in an annexe off the main house. Carlos had told her that his father was partially paralysed after he'd suffered a stroke a year ago. He had been forced to move here from his home in the centre of Toledo and to sell the bakery which had been a family business for four generations.

'Why was your father in hospital?' she asked, as Carlos opened the door and she preceded him out of the study.

'He has been ill with pneumonia. His health is not good. But he hates being inactive and he misses the bakery. He started working there when he was fifteen, and took over running the business when my grandfather retired.'

'Was he disappointed that you didn't go into the family business?'

'I have been a constant disappointment to my father throughout my life.'

Carlos's voice was devoid of emotion, and when Betsy glanced at him she saw his sculpted features were expressionless.

'I bet he's proud of you.' She tried to lighten the atmosphere that suddenly swirled with dark undercurrents. 'After all, you're regarded as the finest sportsman Spain has ever produced and you're a national hero.'

He laughed, but it was not a happy sound, and it hurt Betsy although she couldn't explain why.

'I am no hero,' he said harshly. 'My father would tell you that.'

Ginette came in from the garden with Sebastian just then, and there was no time for Betsy to ask Carlos any more questions. But she sensed his tension as he knocked on the door of his father's private apartment. It surprised her, because Carlos always seemed in complete control of his emotions—*except for that one occasion when he took you to bed and made love to you with a wild passion that spoiled you for any other man,* whispered a voice in her head.

His control had shattered when he had been thrusting inside her, and he'd cursed and told her she had cast a spell on him. And then he'd groaned and slumped on top of her, and she had gloried in her newfound power.

Hastily banishing the erotic images from her mind, Betsy lifted Sebastian out of the pushchair and checked that his face was clean. He looked adorable, in new shorts and a tee shirt, and although she was careful to keep him out of the sun as much as possible his chubby arms and legs were golden-brown.

A nurse came to the door and they followed her into Roderigo's bedroom. The grey-haired man who was propped against the pillows bore little resemblance to Carlos.

Betsy balanced Sebastian on her hip and stepped closer to the bed.

'*Papà*, this is Betsy, and my little boy, Sebastian.' There was fierce pride in Carlos's voice as he introduced his son.

The elderly man stared at Sebastian. *'Se parece a tu madre.'*

'Betsy doesn't speak Spanish,' Carlos told the older man. 'My father said that Sebastian looks like my mother,' he explained to Betsy.

Roderigo stretched out a bony hand and picked up a framed photograph from the bedside table. 'Carlos's mother—my wife Marta. *Dios la bendiga,'* he said thickly, and kissed the photo before he held it out to Betsy.

The woman in the picture was strikingly beautiful, with masses of dark curling hair and sherry-gold eyes. It was easy to see which of his parents Carlos had inherited his good looks from, Betsy thought as she studied the photo.

'Your wife was very pretty,' she said.

Tears filled Roderigo's eyes. 'She died before her time and did not have the chance to see her children become adults or to meet her grandchildren.'

A heavy silence filled the room. *'Papà...'* Carlos murmured.

Roderigo frowned. 'I understand that Sebastian was born over a year ago? Why has it taken you until now to acknowledge your child, Carlos? The story of your secret son is in all the newspapers. Yet again you have brought shame on our family with your playboy reputation and lack of responsibility.'

Beside her, Betsy felt Carlos stiffen. She was startled by his father's accusations and the animosity in Roderigo's voice.

An image flashed into her mind of Carlos kneeling on the stone-flagged floor with his arms wide open to catch Sebastian if he fell, and she remembered the pride in Carlos's voice when he'd introduced his son.

From the minute he'd realised that Sebastian was his, he had offered to support and protect both of them. His father's criticism was unjust, and she was partly to blame, she thought guiltily. She *should* have told Carlos about Sebastian.

'It was my fault that Carlos was unaware he had a child,' she told Roderigo. 'Don't blame your son. There was a misunderstanding which led to us being apart, but now we are going to get married and we are both determined to make a family for Sebastian.'

CHAPTER EIGHT

CARLOS WONDERED IF he had heard correctly. Impossibly, it had sounded as though Betsy was defending him when she'd told his father that *she* had been to blame for keeping Sebastian's birth a secret.

Betsy had wanted to protect him!

Carlos did not know what to make of that, nor of the warmth that curled around his frozen heart. She had no idea how little he deserved her to champion him, he thought bleakly. But his father knew. And Roderigo's tears for his beloved wife had the same impact on Carlos that they always did.

A familiar sense of guilt ripped through him. And now there was new guilt—because he should have stayed and spoken to Betsy after he'd slept with her, instead of rushing back to Spain like a goddamned coward. But he'd been shaken by how she'd made him feel. Scared that she'd made him feel at all when he'd blocked out his emotions for his entire adult life.

How had he thought that this woman was unremarkable? Carlos thought wryly. Betsy never ceased to amaze him. She looked like a ray of sunshine in her yellow dress. The caramel streaks in her hair had lightened to blonde in the sun, and her lush mouth tempted him to claim her lips with his. He had ached to kiss her since he had brought her and his son to Toledo.

But right now Betsy was sitting on the edge of his father's bed, and had Sebastian balanced on her knees. 'He's a good baby, and mostly he sleeps well at night—except when he's cutting a tooth,' she told Roderigo. 'During the day he has so much energy. As soon as he learned to walk, he wanted to run.'

'Carlos was the same when he was young. His mother used to say she could not keep up with him.'

Roderigo chuckled, and Carlos decided that he must have stepped into a parallel universe. He couldn't remember the last time he'd heard his father laugh, but he guessed it had been twenty years ago—before his teenage emotions and hot temper had ruined everything.

Nothing good ever came from making an emotional response to a situation, Carlos brooded. But that wasn't entirely true, he realised as he looked at his beautiful son. Two years ago he had recognised that Betsy was a threat to his peace of mind, but he'd ignored the alarm bells in his head, driven by something more than simply lust when he'd taken her to bed. The result was this unplanned child who had captured his heart.

They stayed for a while longer, until Sebastian started to become fractious and his grandfather looked tired.

'Will you bring *el nene* to visit me tomorrow?' Roderigo asked as Carlos scooped his son off Betsy's lap.

'I'm flying to South Africa later today, to play in an exhibition match, and I'll be away for the rest of the week. When I return, I'll bring Sebastian to see you.'

His father lay back on the pillows. 'So you are still putting tennis first, Carlos. You have brought Betsy and Sebastian to Spain, but now you are about to leave them and travel halfway around the world. Family is precious. You, of all people, should know that.'

'The exhibition match was arranged months ago and the revenue from the ticket sales will go to the Segarra Foundation.'

Carlos's jaw clenched. He did not need his father to remind him that the price of his ruthless ambition had been his mother's life. She had been the lynchpin of the family and the person he'd loved most in the world.

'Carlos's charity does important work for under-privileged children, and I wouldn't want him to cancel a fundraising match,' Betsy told Roderigo. 'But I can bring Sebastian to visit you.'

They left his father's apartment and Carlos carried a by now very fretful Sebastian back to the main part of the house.

'He's hungry—I need to give him his lunch,' Betsy said.

Carlos's suitcase and tennis rackets were by the front door. 'I'll have to go to the airport soon,' he told her. He tightened his arms around his son, hating the prospect of leaving him behind. Ginette came down the stairs. 'Let Ginette give Sebastian his lunch. I want to talk to you,' he told Betsy.

'I thought we'd finished discussing the wedding.' She gave him a puzzled look after the nanny had taken Sebastian to the kitchen.

'In future, when I play exhibition matches abroad, I'll take you and Sebastian with me.' He grimaced. 'I don't want you to think I am abandoning you.'

'I don't think that.' She met his gaze. 'I know how much you care about Sebastian.'

'I care about your feelings too.'

Carlos did not know if he or Betsy was more surprised by his statement. He had spoken unthinkingly, but it was the truth, he realised.

'I want you to be happy here.' He released his breath slowly. 'Why did you tell my father that you had kept Sebastian a secret from me?'

'Because it's true. He blamed you unfairly and it was only right that I explained the situation.' She hesitated before saying in a low voice, 'I'm sorry I didn't tell you that you had a child. You had a right to know.'

The ice around Carlos's heart thawed a little. Betsy's apology meant a lot. But an unanswered question still remained. Would she *ever* have told him that she'd given birth to his son? If fate hadn't sent that journalist to report on the floods in a Dorset village, would Betsy have kept Sebastian a secret for ever?

Since that night at the penthouse, when he had quite literally turned his back on Betsy to stop himself from pulling her into his arms, he had struggled to control his hunger for her. He'd resorted to keeping his distance from her unless they were both spending time with Sebastian.

The evenings when there were just the two of them at dinner had tested his self-control, so he arranged dinner parties or accepted social engagements, telling Betsy that it was a chance for her to meet his friends.

But they were alone now, and it was impossible to ignore the sexual chemistry simmering between them.

Carlos had spent his whole adult life pretending to be someone else, and he'd hidden behind his image of careless playboy for so long that it was a shock to realise that he wasn't really an empty shell. There was hot blood in his veins and a fire in his heart—and this woman was the cause.

'I made a mistake when I kissed you,' he muttered.

Colour ran along her cheekbones, but she said drily, 'It's all right, Carlos. I got the message when we went back to your apartment after the party. I'm not likely to forget how I made a fool of myself.'

He moved closer to her, his eyes on the pulse jerking erratically at the base of her throat. 'It was a mistake because one kiss wasn't enough. Not for me, and not for you. Am I right, *querida*?'

This close, he could see the pale blue veins beneath her creamy skin. He thought again that she was an English rose with a heady fragrance that intoxicated his senses.

She swallowed, and her tongue darted across her lower lip. 'What does *querida* mean?'

'In English I suppose it translates to "darling", or "lover".'

'I'm neither of those things to you.'

'We were lovers once.'

Carlos knew that his driver was waiting outside in the car, to take him to the airport, but he could not tear himself away from Betsy. Her eyes were huge in her face.

'We spent one night together. I'm not sure that qualifies us as lovers,' she whispered.

'I haven't forgotten a single second of that night.' Memories of her lush body and her sweet ardency had haunted him for two goddamned years. He slid his hand beneath her silky hair and clasped her nape as he lowered his head towards hers. 'Have you?'

Her reply was muffled against his lips as he brought his mouth down on hers and kissed her as he'd imagined doing every night for the past three weeks, when he'd tossed and turned in his enormous bed and fought the urge to stride down the hallway to Betsy's room.

He kissed her as if he couldn't have enough of her. And she kissed him back with a fervour that made him so much hungrier, so much more desperate to feel her soft curves beneath him. He pressed his mouth to the sweet hollow at the base of her throat before moving up her neck to explore a delicate ear. She gave a little gasp when he nipped her velvety earlobe, and he laughed and kissed her lips again, revelling in their moist softness.

Carlos forgot that Betsy was the only woman who had ever slipped under his guard, and by the time he remembered he didn't care that she had done so again. He was only aware of the taste of her on his tongue, of the lemon-fresh scent of her hair that spilled around them, and the hard points of her nipples pressed against his chest. He skimmed his hand down her spine and spread his fingers over her bottom, hauling her against the throbbing hardness of his erection.

His brain was entirely focused on how quickly he could get her to a bed, or any flat surface. He doubted they'd make it upstairs to the bedroom, but there was a sitting room across the hallway.

Vaguely, Carlos remembered again that his jet had been fuelled, ready to fly him to South Africa, and that he had a number of business commitments besides the exhibition match in Cape Town.

He pushed his tongue into the heat of Betsy's mouth. To hell with the trip. He would pull out of the exhibition match. Nothing was more vital than satisfying the ravenous beast of his desire for this woman who rocked him to his core.

Carlos froze.

What the hell was he doing? he asked himself as sanity made a belated appearance. Why had he forgotten how easily Betsy could dismantle the barriers that he had put in place when he'd been a traumatised teenager?

Dios! If he hadn't come to his senses he would have had sex with her in a room where any of the household staff might have walked in and seen them. It would have been embarrassing, but worse was the realisation that he'd been prepared to cancel an important trip so that he could stay here with Betsy.

He dropped his arms down to his sides and stepped back from her. She looked as stunned as he felt, and there was still a part of him that wanted to draw her against his chest and simply hold her.

He shoved the thought away, appalled by his loss of control, and made a show of checking the time on his watch. 'I must go,' he murmured, thankful that his voice was level even though his heart was thundering. 'I'll be back in a week.'

An expression that might have been disappointment crossed Betsy's face.

'I'm thinking of taking Sebastian to England while you're away. We left Fraddlington in such a hurry and I'd like to catch up with my friends in the village.'

He frowned. 'I doubt the cottage will be habitable yet.'

'Sarah says that we can stay at the pub.'

'Our wedding is in a week. You will see your friends then. Anyway, I'm using the jet to fly to South Africa,' Carlos said dismissively.

'I don't expect to travel by private jet. There are regular flights to England from Madrid. Why are you objecting?' Betsy looked mutinous. 'You're leaving Sebastian—it doesn't matter if he's here or in Dorset. I miss my old life…the regular customers at the pub and the other mothers at the baby group I used to take Sebastian to. I feel cut off here,' she muttered. 'You can't stop me from taking him home.'

'*This* is his home.'

Carlos raked his hair off his brow, feeling frustration surge through him—and something else that knotted in the pit of his stomach and felt a lot like fear.

'If you disappear with my son there is nowhere in the world you can hide where I won't find you.'

The implied threat in his statement was clearly not lost on Betsy. She bit her lip. 'Do you really think I would abduct Sebastian like my father did to me?' She sighed. 'If our marriage is going to work, you will have to trust me.'

'Trust has to be earned,' he told her curtly. 'I checked with the courier company and their records show that the package I sent to your aunt's house was signed for by "B. Miller". I have proof that you could have called me before Sebastian was born.'

Betsy stared at the mirror and a fairy-tale princess stared back at her. There was an air of unreality about seeing herself in a wedding dress, having vowed since she was eight years old that she never wanted to get married. It did not help that in this particular story the handsome prince had awoken her desire with a kiss before he'd abandoned her—again.

Carlos had arrived back from his trip to South Africa late the previous night, but Betsy had already been in bed and so hadn't seen him. When she'd woken this morning she had heard him in the nursery, talking to Sebastian in Spanish.

Shyness, or bridal nerves—probably a mixture of

both—had stopped her from opening the connecting
door between her room and the nursery. It was supposed to be unlucky for the groom to see the bride before the wedding. Betsy wasn't superstitious, but her
marriage had enough bad omens without tempting fate.

For the past week she had spoken to Carlos on the
phone every day. They had mostly talked about Sebastian, but Carlos had also told her about the series
of exhibition matches he'd played. Betsy had found it
easier to chat to him on the phone, when she was not
physically aware of him. Without the sexual tension
that simmered between them when they were together
she was able to relax, and she'd found herself looking
forward to his calls.

She had decided against taking Sebastian to England
to visit her old friends in the village. It was understand-
able that Carlos did not trust her, she acknowledged.
But she was determined to prove to him that she genuinely regretted not telling him about Sebastian when
he had been born.

Her sense of isolation had increased while Carlos
had been away. None of the household staff spoke more
than a few words of English, and Betsy felt that she
did not belong in a grand house that was served by a
butler, a housekeeper, a cook and several maids. Her
only friend in the whole of Spain was Hector, at the
art supplies shop, and she had found excuses to visit
the shop often, so that she could chat to him and ease
her loneliness.

The grandfather clock on the landing chimed twice

and Betsy's heart missed a beat. Carlos, Sebastian and Ginette the nanny had gone ahead to the church. Now it was time for her to go to her wedding.

She made a last check that her chignon was secure and tucked an escapee curl behind her ear before she picked up her bouquet of palest pink roses. She wished that her parents could be there to see her marry, but yet again they had put their acrimony before her happiness, she thought sadly.

Thinking about their bitter divorce added to her tension. Was she doing the right thing by marrying for convenience rather than love? She thought of the love that Carlos clearly felt for Sebastian, and knew she had no choice.

Carlos had told her that their wedding was to be held in a church in the centre of Toledo, but to Betsy's surprise the driver turned the car in the opposite direction from the city. Soon they were travelling along narrow roads surrounded by wide open plains and vast vineyards and dotted with squat white windmills, beneath a cloudless, blue sky. She knew this landscape of the Castile La Mancha area of Spain was often called the heartland of the country.

After a while they came to a small village, and went through some gates into what seemed to be a private estate. A driveway led to a house that looked like a castle, complete with turrets. Further along the driveway was a whitewashed chapel. The driver brought the car to a halt.

'Are you sure this is the right place?' Betsy asked

him when he held the door open for her to climb out of the car.

'*Si, señorita.*'

She had been expecting a horde of paparazzi, and was surprised to see that there was just one photographer.

A man stepped out of the church and she stared at him in disbelief.

'*Dad?* I didn't think you were coming. Where's Tiffany?'

Betsy knew she would never hear the last of it if her father and his wife attended the wedding, but her mother was left out.

'Hello, honey. You make a beautiful bride.' Drake Miller smiled as he offered her his arm. 'Tiffany is in Paris.' He rolled his eyes. 'She's probably flexing my credit card in the designer stores. Your mother is in the church,' he said casually.

Betsy stopped walking. 'Are you and Mum…okay together? It doesn't look like a very big church.' She tensed, imagining her parents arguing in front of the other wedding guests.

'Carlos told us that we had to put aside our differences at our daughter's wedding, and he's right. Stephanie and I both want to be here for you on your big day,' Drake reassured her as they stepped into the church porch, where it was cool and dark after the bright sunshine outside. 'Your fiancé is an amazing guy and it's obvious that he is madly in love with you.'

Betsy's steps faltered. Carlos did not love her, nor

she him, she reminded herself. Who needed love, anyway? They were marrying for sensible, practical reasons, so that they could both be full-time parents to their son.

Through the doorway she could see the pretty chapel was filled with flowers. In the front pew there was an enormous cerise pink hat which must belong to her mother. She saw Sarah and Mike and other close friends who had flown over from England. On the other side of the nave she recognised some of Carlos's friends, whom she'd met at dinner parties, and she noticed his father in a wheelchair and his sister Graciela, with a man who must be her husband, holding their little boy Miguel. But to Betsy's relief there were certainly not three hundred guests, and not a celebrity in sight.

Finally she turned her gaze to Carlos. He was standing by the altar, his back ramrod-straight, and every few seconds he glanced over his shoulder. He couldn't possibly be feeling nervous, she told herself. His supreme self-confidence was what had helped to make him a world-class tennis champion. He looked devastatingly handsome in a pale grey three-piece suit…the most beautiful man she'd ever seen.

Betsy could not explain the pang her heart gave, nor the tears that pricked her eyes.

At one side of the church a group of musicians were gathered next to the organ. The organist began to play, and the violinists and a cellist picked up their bows. The exquisite notes of Pachelbel's *Canon in D* soared to the rafters as Betsy walked with her father down the aisle.

Carlos had turned his head towards the back of the church when the music had started. His eyes locked on Betsy and he did not look away from her as she made her way towards him. She couldn't fathom the expression that crossed his face, but when she reached his side he said in a hoarse undertone, 'You take my breath away, *mi belleza.*'

The ceremony was simple, but unexpectedly moving. It would be easy to be swept up in the romance of the occasion, thought Betsy, but she knew better than to believe in fairy tales.

Carlos took her hand in his and slid a gold band onto her finger. The priest pronounced them man and wife and her new husband bent his dark head and kissed her while a collective sigh came from the congregation.

It was all a show, Betsy reminded herself. Carlos had been made to look a fool and, worse, callous when the media had discovered he had a secret child. This wedding was to restore his image—but therein was a puzzle.

'Where are the paparazzi you said were bound to be outside the church?' she asked as she and Carlos posed on the steps for the one photographer who was there, taking pictures. 'I thought you wanted a big wedding in the glare of the world's press?'

'But you didn't,' he said softly. 'You were worried that our wedding would be a circus, so I changed the venue and only invited close family and friends to this private chapel, which is owned by a friend of mine. We will have lunch in Sergio's castle, and this evening we will be joined by a couple of hundred other guests for a bigger reception. The paparazzi are banned from entering the estate. We'll choose a few pictures from the photographer and issue them to the press.'

Betsy glanced over at her parents, who were chatting amiably and apparently best friends. 'I can't believe they haven't killed each other,' she murmured. 'What did you do?'

'I reminded them that they had both let you down in the past and warned them that if they upset you today I'd have them forcibly evicted from the wedding.'

'Seriously?'

She stared at him, and her heart flipped when he gave one of his sexy smiles that turned her insides to mush. Sweet heaven! How was she going to survive this? she wondered with a flash of despair. She was touched that he had altered the wedding arrangements to make her happy, and he'd worked a miracle with her parents after she'd admitted that she wished they would attend the wedding.

By the time they returned to Fortaleza Aguila, much later that night, Betsy felt confused. A week ago Carlos had said he could not trust her. But, thanks to him, their wedding day had been a beautiful and memorable event. He had acted the role of loving husband so convincingly that it was difficult to believe he was the same man who had vowed to hunt her to the ends of the earth if she disappeared with Sebastian. The fact that he could even think she would do such a thing reminded her of why she must not fall head over heels in love with him.

'I believe that in England it is traditional for the groom to carry his bride over the threshold,' Carlos said when they alighted from the car and walked towards the house. 'Apparently the ritual goes back to Roman times and was meant to protect the bride from demons that might be in her new home.'

'Luckily we're in Spain.'

Betsy gathered her long skirt in her hands and ran up the steps to the front door. Obscure demons were the least of her concerns. She was far more worried that if Carlos held her in his arms she would be unable to resist pressing her face into his neck and breathing in his evocative male scent.

The door was unlocked, and she pushed it open and sped across the hall as if the devil himself was chasing after her. 'I'm tired and I'm going to bed. Goodnight.'

Upstairs, she stepped quietly into the nursery to check on Sebastian. Ginette had brought him home earlier in the evening, so that he could go to sleep at his usual time. He looked adorable, lying in the cot with his arms above his head, and as usual he had kicked the covers off. Betsy tucked the blanket around him and kissed his cheek.

It had meant a lot to her when she'd watched her parents make a fuss of her baby, especially as it had been the first time her father had met Sebastian. She was stunned that Carlos had gone to such a lot of effort to arrange for her parents to attend the wedding.

But family was important, and now, through their marriage, Sebastian was Carlos's legitimate son and heir.

In her bedroom, she kicked off her shoes and pulled the pins from her chignon before raking her fingers through her hair. It had been a long and emotionally draining day. She frowned as she noticed that the sheets had been stripped from the bed. She would have to remake it, but she had no idea where the bedding was kept and was reluctant to disturb the staff so late at night.

Walking into the en suite bathroom, she discovered that all her toiletries were missing, and back in the bedroom she opened a wardrobe and found it empty.

Betsy was tired, her nerves were frayed, and her temper simmered as she marched down the corridor to Carlos's room. She had never been inside the master bedroom before, and after she'd given a peremptory knock on the door before opening it, her eyes were immediately drawn to the huge four-poster bed in the centre of the room. A gold canopy was draped above the bed, and the gold and black decor gave the room the appearance of a sultan's tent.

Carlos was stretched out on the bed with his arms folded behind his head. He had removed his tie and his shirt was undone to the waist, revealing his impressive abs and that glorious chest, darkly tanned and liberally sprinkled with black body hair. He did not seem surprised to see her, and lifted one dark brow when she walked closer to the bed and glared at him.

'Where are my clothes? Why have all my things been taken out of my room?'

'I asked one of the maids to transfer your belongings here, to the master suite.' Carlos propped himself up on an elbow and waved his hand towards a door. 'Through there is your own bathroom and dressing room. Now that you are my wife you will share my bedroom with me.'

His wolfish smile caused Betsy's womb to contract, and she realised that the biggest threat she faced was not her too-hot-to-handle husband but her irresistible attraction to him when he patted the mattress and murmured, 'Come to bed, *querida.*'

CHAPTER NINE

'YOU SAID THAT our marriage would be a partnership and we would make decisions together.'

Betsy grabbed hold of the nearest bedpost for support as a terrible weakness invaded her body. In her traitorous imagination she pictured herself and Carlos lying on the bed, their naked limbs entwined.

'I have no intention of sleeping in your bedroom with you,' she told him—and herself—firmly. 'In the morning you can ask the staff to return my clothes to my room and remake my bed. But for tonight I'll use this as a cover.'

She snatched up the black velvet throw that was draped across the bottom of Carlos's bed. Her temper fizzed when he said nothing, just lay sprawled on the gold satin bedspread like a demigod—too handsome to be a mere mortal.

'We *will* discuss issues as they arise. But I did previously mention that we would share a bedroom after we married,' he reminded her.

'I didn't realise that you meant on our actual wedding night,' she muttered. 'You also "mentioned" that we would have a sexual relationship at some point. Are you going to demand that I have sex with you tonight?'

'Of course not.' An expression of horror crossed his face. '*Dios*, you can't really believe I would try to force myself on you?' He sounded as though he was struggling to control some violent emotion.

Betsy sighed. 'No, I don't believe that.' Her shock was fading, and she knew with complete certainty that she was safe with Carlos. 'But why is it so important for us to share a room?'

'Can you imagine how the paparazzi would react if they found out that we slept apart?' he demanded. 'The tabloids would speculate that our marriage is already over or that our wedding was a stunt.'

She frowned. 'How would the tabloids find out details about our personal lives?'

'I believe that my household staff are trustworthy,' Carlos told her, 'but it only takes a careless remark to spark a rumour. The maids will know if we are sleeping in separate rooms. I won't risk details of our private lives being aired by the gutter press.'

Betsy was about to say that it was a fanciful idea. But then she remembered that when she was a child an au pair had leaked information to the media about her parents' explosive arguments. Every gory detail of her father's infidelity and her mother's out-of-control spending had been documented and sold to a newspaper. The au pair had only been discovered when she'd left her notebook open in the kitchen and Betsy's mother had seen it.

'I wouldn't care what the press printed about us,' she insisted. But it wasn't true. She hated the thought of her personal life being made public again.

'I don't think you would enjoy being constantly harassed by the paparazzi about the state of our marriage. And it's not just the newspapers. My father lives in the house, and he would soon find out if our relationship was not the happy marriage that we have led him and other members of our families to believe. He adores Sebastian, and if he has reason to think there is a rift between us he'll worry that you might leave and take his grandson away.'

'I've told you I will never do that.' Betsy hesitated, then said, 'I've gained the impression that your relationship with Roderigo is strained. Why is that?'

Carlos stiffened. 'It is a private matter between my father and me.'

'It might help to talk,' she murmured. 'I am part of your family now, and—'

'Leave it,' he ordered curtly. 'There are things that you don't understand.'

Betsy felt a pang of hurt that he was shutting her out. She moved her gaze from the huge bed and glanced at a high-backed armchair. She did not relish trying to sleep on that.

'I didn't expect that we would share a bedroom immediately we were married.'

He stood up and curved his fingers over Betsy's

hand, where it was clinging to the bedpost. 'I won't expect anything from you that you are not willing to give. But I know you want me, *querida*.' His voice deepened and his eyes gleamed like molten gold as he lifted his other hand and smoothed her hair back from her flushed face. 'And I want you, my beautiful wife. Two years ago, neither of us could ignore the attraction we felt for each other. That chemistry is still there, hotter and more potent than ever.'

She shook her head, but the faintly sardonic expression in his eyes said that he did not believe her denial. His gaze lowered to the hard peaks of her nipples, outlined beneath the silk bodice of her wedding dress.

'Your body betrays you, *mi belleza*.'

He stepped closer, and his warm breath grazed her cheek. His mouth was mere centimetres away from hers, but he did not kiss her as she longed for him to do. He captured her free hand in his and lifted it up so that he could press his lips to the gold band sitting next to the exquisite diamond on her finger.

Sensation shot through her as he turned her palm over and kissed her wrist, where her pulse was beating erratically. He feathered kisses along her arm to the crook of her elbow and nipped the delicate skin there very gently with his teeth, sending sparks of fire through her veins. When he lifted his head she released her breath on a soft sigh that turned to a gasp as he licked his way along her collarbone and trailed his lips up her throat and over the sensitive underside of her jaw.

Surely he would kiss her mouth now? He was so close, so tempting. She wanted to spear her fingers into the dark silk of his hair and tug his head closer until his lips were on hers. The ache inside her was sharpest between her legs, and she was conscious of the damp heat of her feminine arousal.

Carlos released her hand and she hovered it over his naked chest. She wanted to touch his warm skin. He smelled of spicy cologne and raw male, and her womanly body responded instinctively to his potency.

'Touch me.'

His voice was thick with desire. Betsy swayed towards him and skimmed her fingers over his chest, feeling the abrasion of his body hair beneath her fingertips. He was the most beautiful man in the world. He could have any woman he wanted, but he wanted *her*. She recognised the hunger in the feral glitter in his eyes and heard it in the raggedness of his breath.

'Come to bed and let me make love to you,' he said roughly. 'We are married now.'

So they might as well have sex?

Was that what Carlos thought?

Cold reality replaced the sensual heat that had fogged Betsy's brain and she snatched her hand away from him. 'But you don't trust me.'

He had made that clear before he'd gone to South Africa, when he'd accused her of lying about not receiving the bracelet that he insisted he had sent her.

Betsy had tried to contact Aunt Alice's son, to ask him if a package had arrived at the house in London after she'd moved out. But, frustratingly, Lee's wife had told her that he was away on a fishing trip in a remote part of Scotland where he couldn't use his phone.

Carlos raked a hand through his hair. *'Querida...'*

'Don't!' she choked. 'I'm not your darling.'

He had the power to destroy her, and the realisation terrified her. If she gave herself to him he would know how much he affected her. She did not trust herself to be able to hide her feelings. She wasn't in love with him, but what she felt was deeper than lust and that made her vulnerable.

'I'm not going to have sex with you.'

His gaze narrowed on her face and she sensed his frustration. But after a few seconds he moved away from her and she released her breath slowly.

'I need to get changed,' she told him. 'I can't sleep in my wedding dress.' She hoped he wouldn't hear the wobble in her voice.

Why not just accept the wedding night Carlos is offering? whispered a voice in her head. Sex without strings would set the tone for their marriage and satisfy her physical craving for him.

But an instinct for self-preservation held her back. He made her feel as defenceless now as she'd felt two years ago. She'd cried into her pillow every night for weeks after he'd returned to Spain. But then she'd found out she was pregnant, and she'd ditched her romantic dreams for the reality of being a single mother.

Carlos crossed the room and opened the door that he'd indicated a few minutes ago. Betsy stepped into a walk-in wardrobe, beyond which was another door to her own bathroom. The new clothes she'd bought since she'd arrived in Spain were on hangers or folded on shelves. She searched the room and eventually found the few possessions she'd brought from England. After taking off her wedding dress she went into the bathroom to wash her face and brush her teeth.

Five minutes later she returned to the bedroom, and her heart lurched when she saw Carlos already in bed, leaning against the pillows. His chest was bare and the sheet was draped across his hips. The thought that he might be completely naked tested her resolve. How would she get to sleep, knowing that all that testosterone was a few feet away from her?

'Madre de Dios!' He sat up straighter when he saw her. 'What the hell are you wearing?'

'My pyjamas. I bought them last winter, to keep out the cold.' Made of thick flannelette, in a violent purple check pattern, they were hideous, but they had been very practical when she'd had to get up to Sebastian in the middle of the night. She would probably boil, wearing them now in the heat of a Spanish summer, but it was worth the risk, she decided. From Carlos's expression it seemed the unflattering pyjamas had cooled his desire, and Betsy told herself she was relieved.

'Your choice of nightwear is not quite what I'd imagined my bride would wear on our wedding night,' he said drily.

Taking a deep breath, Betsy pulled back the sheet on the other side of the bed and slid beneath it. She couldn't get it out of her mind that he might be stark naked. There was a long bolster pillow behind her head, and she placed it down the centre of the bed before she switched off her bedside lamp.

Carlos muttered something in Spanish and turned off his own lamp.

Betsy blinked as her eyes adjusted to the darkness. 'I don't suppose you even imagined your wedding night, as you are on record stating that you never wanted to get married.' She sighed. 'Nor did I. We had a one-night stand, and that's all it should have been. But, un-beknown to either of us, when you returned to Spain I had conceived your baby.'

The mattress dipped as Carlos moved and his face appeared above the bolster. 'Do you regret having Se-bastian? I've never asked how you felt about becoming a mother, but I assume you wanted him?'

'Of course I don't regret having him. He's the best thing that has ever happened in my life. I can't begin to explain how much I love him.' Her voice thickened with emotions that she couldn't supress. 'I agreed to this ridiculous marriage for Sebastian's sake.'

Betsy's eyes brimmed with tears and she was glad of the dark as they slipped unchecked down her cheeks. She swallowed hard, but a sob escaped her.

Carlos leaned closer and his gold-flecked eyes glit-tered in his shadowed face. 'Are you *crying*?'

'N...no.' Her voice cracked on the lie. He swore, and she sensed he was shocked. Embarrassment added to her misery. She couldn't explain why she felt so overwhelmed, but it was a combination of things: seeing her parents behaving civilly to each other, watching Sebastian playing with his cousin Miguel and realising that he already seemed more Spanish than English...

But the main reason why her emotions felt like a wrung-out dishcloth was the memory of Carlos being so attentive to her throughout their wedding day, and holding her close when they'd danced the first dance at the evening reception. She'd almost been fooled into thinking that he cared about her.

More tears filled her eyes and she covered her face with her forearm, feeling exposed and stupid.

For a heartbeat Carlos did not move, but then he grabbed the bolster and hurled it off the bed. 'Come,' he murmured, reaching for her and drawing her across the mattress.

The warmth of his body was irresistible, and Betsy succumbed without a struggle. She wasn't sure if she was relieved or disappointed when her hand brushed against the silk boxers he was wearing.

'Don't cry, *pequeña*.'

He spoke softly, as if she was a small child needing to be comforted, and stroked his hand over her hair. She had seen his gentleness with Sebastian, but now he was being kind to her, and she cried harder.

'Why is our marriage ridiculous?' he asked.

'You...hate me.'

'I don't hate you.' He exhaled heavily. 'I admit I was angry at first, but I have never hated you.'

She sniffed. 'You can't forgive me for keeping your son a secret.'

Once again Carlos hesitated for a heartbeat before he said gruffly, 'I understand why you were afraid to tell me. Your childhood experiences when your parents wanted you to choose between them made you determined to protect Sebastian.' He slid his finger beneath her chin and tilted her face to his. 'We may not have married for conventional reasons, but I believe we can make it work, *querida*.' He rolled onto his back, taking her with him, and tucked her head on his shoulder. Go to sleep now. Things will seem better in the morning.'

Carlos meant, of course, that they had not married for love—and she was fine with that, Betsy assured herself. Her parents had proved that love could be a destructive emotion. And it seemed as though he had forgiven her for keeping Sebastian a secret, but she still felt guilty. Somehow, they had to make a success of their marriage for their son's sake.

Her thoughts blurred as she slipped into sleep. She didn't wish that Carlos would fall in love with her. Really, she didn't.

'Have you seen my wife?' Carlos asked the nanny, who had just emerged from the nursery.

'I believe she has gone into the city. She often goes shopping for a couple of hours in the afternoon. Sebastian has dropped his morning nap, but he still sleeps after he's had his lunch,' Ginette explained. 'If I'd known you were back I would have kept him up so that you could see him,' she said apologetically. 'Betsy thought you wouldn't return from your business trip until later this evening.'

'I'll spend time with him when he wakes up.'

Carlos stepped quietly into the nursery and leaned over the cot to kiss his son's downy cheek. His heart swelled with love for Sebastian and he gave a rueful sigh. In his careless bachelor days he had been adamant that he did not want children. But now he had a child and would willingly give his life for his precious little boy.

Leaving Sebastian to nap, Carlos walked down the corridor and into the master bedroom. Betsy's scent was everywhere in the house, but it was strongest here, in the bedroom they shared, and his gut clenched. He slung his jacket on the chair and tugged off his tie. Picking up his phone, he logged on to internet banking and checked the account that Betsy withdrew money and made payments from. The balance had not changed in the two weeks since he'd given her a bank card in her married name.

Carlos was fairly sure that Betsy did not have any savings of her own, so how did she pay for whatever she was buying on her shopping trips?

He sat on the edge of the bed, wondering how much longer their marriage could continue to be a Cold War, with both of them entrenched on either side of a goddamned bolster. Cursing, he grabbed the bolster off the bed and threw it out into the corridor. He'd tell the maid to get rid of it.

But the barrier between him and Betsy was more than just the pillow that she placed down the centre of the bed every night. Her tears on their wedding night had made him feel uncomfortable. The evidence of her vulnerability had exacerbated his guilt that he'd forced her into a marriage which she had openly admitted she did not want.

But what other choice had either of them had? Carlos brooded. He had been utterly determined that his son would be legitimate. For Sebastian's sake, he and Betsy must try to make a success of their marriage, but so far it was a disaster for which he must accept most of the blame.

His plan had been that they would have a short period of time while they adjusted to living together, and that this would lead naturally to them beginning a sexual relationship. But Carlos was being hampered by two things. The first was his rampant desire for Betsy, that made it impossible for him to be near her without wanting to haul her off to bed and make love to her until they were both sated. The second but greater problem was his discovery on their wedding night that she could easily be hurt—by him.

He wanted to have sex with her, but he did not want emotional sex. It wasn't his thing. And Carlos sensed that Betsy would want more than he was prepared to give her. Wasn't that always the way with women? he thought frustratedly. He had given Betsy his name, his home and his promise of commitment. But when she'd cried, he'd felt as if his insides had been ripped out. He'd wanted to protect her.

Por Dios! His track record was not good in that department. And so he had kept his distance from his new wife. He'd gone away on business trips and spent several nights at the penthouse in Madrid, so that he didn't have to lie beside Betsy, fantasising about unbuttoning the pyjamas that she wore like a suit of armour. She seemed equally keen to avoid him, and when he was at home she spent a lot of time in her old bedroom.

Carlos decided that he needed to try a new approach. They had done everything the wrong way around. They'd had a baby, then they'd got married, but they had never had a chance to get to know each other. He remembered that Betsy had mentioned she would like to visit the El Greco museum in Toledo. He would meet her and take her there, he thought as he picked up his phone and called her.

She did not answer, nor reply to his text. But Carlos was a man on a mission as he went downstairs and found his driver in the kitchen.

'Do you know which shops Señora Segarra intended to go to?' he asked Pablo.

'*Sí. La señora* always visits the art supplies shop on Calle Santa Tomé.' For some reason the driver looked uncomfortable.

Carlos remembered that Betsy had painted pets' portraits when she'd lived in Dorset. He was puzzled that Pablo avoided his gaze. 'Does she go to the art shop often?'

'Very often. And only to that place. She has asked me to collect her in one hour.'

'Give me directions to the art shop,' Carlos requested. 'I'll drive myself there to meet my wife.'

It did not take him long to reach the city walls, and he parked in a car park that most tourists hadn't discovered. The narrow, cobbled streets of Toledo were thronged with visitors in the summer, but the art shop was tucked down an alleyway where few people ventured.

Carlos walked through the door and glanced at the artists' materials displayed rather haphazardly around the shop. There was no one behind the serving counter, but there was a bell that had a sign next to it saying *Presiona*.

At the rear of the shop was a door which opened on to a courtyard. Carlos felt an odd sensation, as if his heart had performed a somersault, when he saw Betsy through the doorway. Her hair was loose on her shoulders and shone like raw silk in the sunshine. She'd gained a light golden tan since coming to Spain, and she seemed to grow sexier and more beautiful every day.

She was standing by a small fountain in the courtyard, and with her was a long-haired young man whose arms were covered in tattoos and a couple of other arty types. Someone was strumming on a guitar and there was a low hum of easy conversation.

Betsy suddenly gave a shriek as Tattoo Guy splashed her with water. 'That's not fair!' She laughed and shook her hair back from her face. Her wet shirt clung to her breasts—a fact that had not gone unnoticed by Tattoo Guy.

Something hot and rancid flared in Carlos's gut. Possessiveness ran like wildfire through his veins as the sound of Betsy's laughter drifted into the shop. She had never laughed or been so carefree with *him*, he thought darkly. The sense of betrayal felt like a knife through his heart. She was his *wife*, goddammit, and the mother of his son. They were meant to be a family.

It struck him then how badly he wanted a family to replace the one he had destroyed. But his guilt had made him think that he did not deserve one, and he acknowledged that he had kept Betsy at a distance because she was the only woman who threatened to dismantle the barriers he had erected around his emotions.

Betsy looked at her watch. Pablo would come to collect her soon, and her heart sank at the prospect of returning to Fortaleza Aguila. Of course she loved being with Sebastian, but she wished she could meet some other mothers with toddlers, so that he could mix with children of his age. She thought wistfully of the baby group in Fraddlington, where she'd made some good friends.

Coming to see Hector at the art shop made a welcome change, though, from the stiff formality of the dinner parties she attended with Carlos. None of his close friends had children, and the women were all incredibly glamourous. Betsy found them intimidating.

Her skin prickled and a sixth sense made her turn her head in the direction of the shop. Her heart gave a jolt when she saw Carlos step into the courtyard. To anyone who did not know him he'd appear to be relaxed. But the hard gleam in his eyes and the tense line of his jaw warned her that he was furious.

She was conscious that her wet shirt was clinging to her breasts. Hector had just been fooling around, but she had a feeling that Carlos would not see it that way. His eyes roamed over her short denim skirt before returning to her breasts. Predictably, she felt her nipples jerk to attention. This inability to control her reaction to her husband was one reason why she spent as little time alone with him as possible.

Hector and his friends Antonio and Sofia were staring at Carlos with awed expressions. Even though he had retired from playing tennis professionally, he was still a national hero in Spain.

'*Holà!* Can I help you?' Hector said in Spanish.

'I'm here to take my wife home.' The Jaguar smiled, baring his teeth.

Hector shot Betsy a rueful look. 'You forgot to mention that your husband is the great Carlos Segarra.'

She bit her lip, unable to explain that she had wanted to make friends on her own merits, rather than impress people by revealing who she was married to.

'Come, *querida*,' Carlos ordered.

Betsy bristled at his arrogance, but his slashing frown warned her against making a scene. 'See you soon,' she told Hector, and swept past Carlos without looking at him.

When they emerged into the street he caught hold of

her arm and steered her to where he'd parked his car. Betsy's temper fizzed.

'There's no need to manhandle me,' she muttered, glancing at his scowling face. 'What's biting you?' she demanded when he opened the door of his sports car and she slid into the passenger seat.

'This discussion will wait until we are home,' he growled.

Betsy felt like a naughty schoolgirl, and when they reached the house she half expected Carlos to march her into his study.

She walked quickly ahead of him towards the stairs. 'I'm going to get changed.'

She stopped at the nursery to check on Sebastian and found he was still asleep. Ginette looked up from her book. 'I'll pick him up when he stirs,' the nanny whispered.

In the master bedroom, Betsy stripped off her damp shirt and dropped it in the laundry basket. Carlos's voice sounded from the doorway and she spun round to face him. Her pink lacy bra was no more revealing that the bikini top he'd seen her wearing in the pool, she told herself, but she still felt self-conscious that she was half undressed, and crossed her arms over her chest.

He stepped into the room and shut the door with suppressed violence. 'You are not to see him again.'

She blinked. 'Who?'

'Your boyfriend with the body art.'

'Hector is a friend—he's not my *boyfriend*. I can't believe you're accusing me…'

'I saw the way he looked at you.' Carlos's jaw clenched. 'You were flirting with him and laughing.'

'I wasn't *flirting*. Hector has a girlfriend.' She threw her hands up in exasperation. 'And laughing isn't a crime. The only time I *feel* like laughing is when I'm with the friends I've made at the art shop. Hector lived in England for a while, and it's such a relief to be able to talk to him without a Spanish phrasebook.'

Betsy's shoulders slumped.

'I've been so lonely since I came to live in Spain… The staff keep themselves to themselves. We socialise with your friends and I have nothing in common with them.' She could not hide the tremor in her voice. 'I'm trying to learn Spanish, but it's hard speaking a new language and living in a new country where I'm an outsider. The staff run the house and we have a nanny to look after Sebastian. It feels like I don't have a role here.'

'Your role is as my wife,' Carlos said tersely.

'You never wanted a wife and our marriage is a…a farce. You're hardly ever at home.' Betsy had opened the floodgates now, and her unhappiness and dissatisfaction poured out. 'How dare you accuse me of flirting with Hector when *you* have spent more nights at your penthouse than here with me in the bedroom you insisted we share? I don't suppose you sleep alone at your bachelor pad in Madrid.'

Carlos swore. 'Do you think I have a mistress?'

'I don't know *what* to think.' It crucified her to imagine him making love to another woman. 'You said you wanted to make our marriage work, but we don't spend time together or have any kind of relationship. At least Hector is interested in me. And he's supportive of my pet portrait business, which happens to be doing very well—as I would have told you if you ever paid me any attention.'

Carlos strode across the room and halted in front of her. He was so close that Betsy felt the warmth of his body through his black silk shirt. His male scent evoked a molten heat low in her pelvis.

'I don't have a mistress,' he ground out. 'I haven't slept with any woman since you.'

Her eyes widened and he gave her a sardonic look.

'It's the truth. I couldn't get you out of my mind for two years.'

He lowered his head and she felt his breath graze her cheek.

'If you want my attention you only have to ask, *mi belleza*,' he said roughly, before he claimed her mouth and kissed her with fierce possession.

CHAPTER TEN

THERE WAS FURY in his kiss and Betsy's temper blazed. Anger and desire were an explosive mix. She welcomed the thrust of his tongue inside her mouth as she parted her lips beneath his and kissed him with all the pent-up frustration that had simmered inside her for weeks.

Every night, when she'd kept to her side of the mattress and Carlos had stayed on the opposite side, she had lacked the nerve to move the wretched bolster from the centre of the bed. She had been responsible for putting the barrier between them and she understood that he would not remove it.

Carlos was proud, but he was also a virile male, and his hunger for her was evident when she pressed herself against him and felt the hard length of his arousal nudge her thigh. A shudder of longing ran through her and she tugged open the buttons on his shirt and skimmed her hands over his bare chest. His olive skin was warm, and she loved the springy feel of his dark chest hair against her palms as she explored the ridges of his powerful muscles.

He muttered something in Spanish, and then the world tilted as he lifted her off her feet and dumped her unceremoniously on the bed. Betsy thought she should care that he was the most arrogant man she'd ever met. But he was Carlos, and she could not fool herself any longer that she had any control where this man was concerned.

He was her husband, and yet not her husband. Not in any way that counted. She had turned him down on their wedding night because she had been afraid that he would destroy her if she had sex with him. Now she knew he would destroy her if he did *not* make love to her.

He knelt on the bed and loomed over her. 'Am I paying you enough attention now, *querida*?'

His eyes glittered as Betsy traced her fingers over his hard jaw. She was so weak for him. But instead of seeing desire as a weakness, perhaps there was strength in admitting what she wanted.

'Not enough attention,' she said huskily. 'I want more.'

'You will be the death of me,' he muttered as he slipped his hands beneath her back and unclipped her bra. He tossed it aside and captured her wrists in one of his hands, holding them above her head. Dull colour winged along his cheekbones as he studied her bare breasts. Betsy felt her nipples grow tight beneath his intent gaze. His features sharpened with a predatory hunger that made the ache in her pelvis so much worse—or better?

She made a choked sound when he bent his head to

one breast and flicked his tongue across its rosy peak. Sensation spiralled through her and she arched towards him as he tormented her with delicate licks across her nipple. She tried to tug her hands free, but he held her pinioned against the mattress while he drew her nipple into his mouth.

Why fight him when this was what she craved?

His mouth was creating havoc on her body. He released her hands and she sank them into his hair as he moved across to her other breast and sucked the hot, tight peak. Pleasure arced down to her feminine core and she felt the slippery wetness of her arousal.

Carlos trailed his lips over her abdomen and at the same time shoved her denim skirt up to her waist. He drew lazy patterns on her inner thighs with his fingers, but to her frustration he held back from touching her where she longed to feel him.

His eyes gleamed hard and bright as he trapped her gaze. 'Have you had enough of my attention yet, *mi bella esposa*?'

'Not nearly enough.' The words burst from her, urgent and needy. But she didn't care. She couldn't pretend that he did not affect her. The fire inside her only burned this hot for him.

His mouth twisted, but there was no triumph in his smile, rather a tenderness that she understood would be her downfall. Her thoughts scattered as he stared at the scrap of pink lace that covered her femininity. His smile became wicked as he ran his finger over the damp panel between her legs. And then he simply pulled her panties off and pushed her legs apart.

There was something shockingly intimate about lying splayed open to his hungry gaze. But she did not feel vulnerable. She felt empowered when Carlos groaned, and she knew—*she knew*—that he was at the mercy of their tumultuous desire just as she was.

He moved down the bed so that his shoulders were between her thighs, and she gave a start as she realised what he intended to do. Her protest died on her lips when he ran his tongue along her inner thigh, higher and higher, until he was *there* where she was hottest and neediest. Betsy gave a low cry when he put his mouth on her and bestowed upon her the most intimate caress of all.

It was too much…not enough. She wanted more.

Her hips bucked and she gasped as he explored her with his tongue and simultaneously pressed his thumb against the tight nub of her clitoris.

The effect was cataclysmic. Pleasure that was indescribable, so intense she could hardly bear it, rolled through her in wave after rippling wave as her internal muscles clenched and released in the sweetest rhythm.

She remembered that first time two years ago, when he had brought her to orgasm with his fingers. While she had still been in the throes of her climax he'd pressed forward and eased his erection into her.

Now, as then, the beauty of his lovemaking brought tears to her eyes. She tried to blink them away as Carlos sat back on his haunches and surveyed the evidence of her complete capitulation: her skirt rucked up around her waist and her thighs spread wide open.

Betsy quickly brushed her hand over her eyes before she reached for Carlos's belt buckle. She could tell from the rigid set of his jaw that he was holding himself back, but she wanted everything he could give her and she wanted to give him pleasure in return.

He caught the errant tear on her cheek with his thumb and swore. 'I lost my temper.' His voice was harsh with self-recrimination.

She recalled their argument after he'd followed her into the bedroom. They had both been angry, but it had been an anger born of frustration that had quickly turned into desire.

'Carlos…'

But her hands dropped away from him as he leapt off the bed and stared at her. He swore again, and tugged her skirt into place so that it covered her nakedness.

'I never, *ever* allow myself to lose my temper,' he said tightly. 'But when I watched you laughing with another man I saw red. I wanted to kill him.' Carlos raked both his hands through his hair. 'I was furious. I couldn't control my anger.'

'If I had seen you with another woman I would probably have reacted the same way,' Betsy murmured. 'Nothing happened just now that I didn't want to happen. I wanted you.' She flushed. 'I still do.'

He finished buttoning his shirt. 'Don't make excuses for me. That makes it worse,' he grated. 'When I'm with you I lose control.'

He said it as if it was a bad thing. As if he bitterly regretted the passion that had exploded between them.

He strode over to the door and paused on his way out of the room to look back at Betsy. 'It won't happen again,' he told her savagely, and then he was gone.

Carlos could not forget Betsy's stricken expression, nor forgive himself. The shimmer of tears in her eyes and her attempt to hide her distress as she'd brushed her hand over her face had jolted him to his senses. He knew he should not have followed her up to the bedroom. It would have been safer if he'd gone to his study and brought his anger under control before going to find her. Perhaps if he had they would have had a calm discussion about the problems with their marriage.

But a wild fury had overwhelmed him as he'd remembered how happy and relaxed Betsy had been with that guy at the art shop. If he hadn't known better he might have thought the corrosive sensation in his gut was jealousy. But nothing excused the fact that he had kissed her in anger. Had he learned nothing from the past, when his temper had caused such devastation?

He had promised himself that he would wait until Betsy was ready to consummate their marriage. Yes, she had asked for his attention, but instead of talking to her he had seduced her.

Full of self-loathing, he strode down to the gym in the basement of the house, changed into sports gear and jumped onto the treadmill. Since he was fourteen, physical exercise had been his method of temporarily blocking out the voices of his demons, who never allowed him to forget his guilt. His superb athleticism had made him a tennis world champion, but training for hours and pushing his body to its limits also gave him control over his emotions.

For two hours he ran, lifted weights and slammed his fists into a punchbag. But nothing silenced the recriminations in his head when he remembered that Betsy had said she'd felt lonely since he had brought her to Spain.

Before leaving Dorset they had gone to the pub in Fraddlington, so that she could say goodbye to her friend Sarah. The pub had been damaged in the flood, but many of the villagers had come to help clean up the mess and everyone there had known Betsy by name. Carlos realised that she missed the close-knit community she had left behind.

He had done little to help her settle into her new home, he thought guiltily. He'd introduced her to his friends, but Betsy was shy and there was the language barrier. It was no wonder that she had become friendly with this tattooed guy who spoke English and shared her interest in art.

Breathing hard from physical exertion, he threw off his boxing gloves and picked up his phone to look on the internet. Betsy had said that her pet portrait business was doing well, and when he typed in her name he was directed to her website.

Carlos knew a little about art, and nothing about domestic pets, but it was apparent from Betsy's online portfolio and her many glowing reviews that she was a talented artist and her clientele list was growing.

She hadn't told him about her work—but he'd never asked her about it, he thought guiltily. He had been so intent on fighting his desire for her that he'd missed his chances to understand the fascinating woman he had married.

After he'd showered, Carlos went to the nursery and found Betsy playing with Sebastian. She blushed when he walked into the room, and avoided his gaze as she scooped the toddler up.

'Look, poppet, your *papà* has come to play with you,' she said to Sebastian in a fiercely bright voice. 'You can take over for a while,' she told Carlos as she handed him his son. 'He might be persuaded to sit in his buggy—you could take him for a walk in the olive groves, where there's some shade under the trees.'

'We need to talk,' he murmured as she walked over to the door.

She rolled her eyes. 'Because that went *so* well the last time we tried it.'

His jaw clenched. 'Betsy…'

'Did I do something wrong?' she asked huskily. 'Is that why you had a face like thunder when you walked out? You are the only man I've been with…maybe you find my lack of experience a turn-off?'

'*Dios*, no.' Once again he realised how vulnerable she was. 'It wasn't you. It's me.'

She gave him a wry look. 'Those words are usually a prelude to "We'll be better off apart".'

'I don't think that.' His stomach hollowed. 'Do you?'

'The truth is, I don't know,' she choked.

Later, after Carlos had taken Sebastian for a walk and fed him his tea, Ginette offered to give the little boy his bath. Carlos knocked on the door of the room adjoining the nursery, which had been Betsy's bedroom before their marriage.

Her smile faded when she saw him. 'I thought you were Ginette.' She glanced down at her paint-spattered shirt. 'I'll just get cleaned up before I come and see to Sebastian's bedtime routine.'

'Ginette is bathing him. Can I come in?'

She shrugged and stepped aside for him to enter the room. 'It's a bit of a mess. I'm trying to finish a portrait that a client commissioned as a wedding anniversary present for her husband.'

Carlos saw the canvas propped against the back of a chair next to the window. The dressing table was covered with paints and brushes. To his inexpert eye, the painting of a German Shepherd looked to be completed.

'The light is no good in here in the afternoon.' Betsy frowned as she stared at the painting. 'I can't get Ludo's eyes right…' She sifted through several photos of the dog.

'I've wondered how you persuade your subjects to sit still while you paint them,' Carlos said, aware of Betsy's surprise that he was showing an interest in her work. 'I checked out your website. Your paintings are amazing.'

She flushed. 'Thank you. I ask clients to take high-resolution photos of their pet so that I can create the best likeness.' She picked up a brush and focused her attention back on the German Shepherd.

'Why do you paint animal portraits? Do you never have people as your subjects?'

'I prefer to paint animals—especially dogs—because they're so honest and uncomplicated. When you look into a dog's eyes you can see its soul, and the love they can give is unconditional.' She sighed. 'When I was a child, we had a dog. He was a miniature white poodle that my father had bought for my mother. She named him Theodore and made a huge fuss of him for a week. But he went out of favour after he chewed one of her shoes and I was allowed to have his basket in my bed-room. I called him Teddy and I adored him.'

Carlos frowned. 'I sense that this story doesn't have a happy ending?'

'In the divorce my father insisted that he had paid for the dog and so should be allowed to keep him. He didn't really want Teddy—he did it to annoy my mother. Then Dad moved to Canada and took the dog with him. When I went there to visit, I couldn't wait to see Teddy, but my father said he had escaped from the garden and been killed. He ran into the road and was hit by a car.'

Betsy's voice was carefully controlled as she re-counted this story from her childhood. Her parents had no idea how much damage they had done to their daughter, Carlos brooded as he watched her pick up a brush and continue to work on the painting.

She stepped back and surveyed what she had done. 'That's better. He looks like Ludo now.'

Carlos studied the portrait. With a few brushstrokes Betsy had captured the German Shepherd's expression perfectly.

'Your parents' relationship has understandably made you wary,' he said. 'But our marriage is not the same as theirs.'

'At least they liked each other to start with…'

He heard the catch in her voice and his heart clenched. 'I like you, *querida*.'

'That's not the impression you gave this afternoon.'

He looked at her stiff shoulders and sensed her hurt pride. 'I would like us to go away together—just the two of us. It's traditional for newlyweds to have a honeymoon,' he murmured when she stared at him.

'What about Sebastian?'

'Ginette is happy to look after him. And my sister has agreed to bring Miguel and come and stay at the house while we are away. Graciela loves Sebastian, and the two boys enjoy each other's company.'

Betsy stared at him. 'You really want us to have a honeymoon? When would we go?'

Carlos discovered that he had been holding his breath while he waited for her response. He exhaled slowly. 'We're leaving in ten minutes. A maid has packed a bag for you.' He forestalled the protest he could see she was about to make. 'It's only a short flight to Palma and we'll arrive before sunset.'

The sun was sliding into the sea when Carlos drove into a small fishing village on Mallorca. Betsy glanced at him and her heart gave a familiar pang. He'd opened the sunroof and his dark hair was tousled by the breeze. His aviator sunglasses were the epitome of style, and his pale denim shirt was open at the throat. He was so sexy it hurt her to look at him, so she turned her attention to the island's stunning scenery.

They passed through the village and a few minutes later he drove up a narrow lane and stopped the car outside a pretty stone cottage with cream shutters at the windows and ivy growing over the walls.

'Our honeymoon destination: Casita Viola,' he said.

He sounded relaxed and his wide smile stole Betsy's breath.

'I was expecting a glamorous five-star hotel,' she murmured.

He tensed and looked away from her. 'You're disappointed? We can go to a hotel if you like.'

'No, it's beautiful here.' She climbed out of the car and turned to admire the view of a crystal-clear sea beyond the white cliffs.

'Those steps lead down to a private beach,' Carlos told her, pointing to some steps carved into the cliff.

The sky was streaked with pink and gold from the setting sun, and the air was filled with the scents of lavender and frangipani which she could see grew in the garden. There was a sense of peace here, Betsy thought as she followed Carlos into the cottage.

Inside, it was full of rustic charm, with exposed stone walls and tiled floors.

'My mother grew up here,' he told her. 'She moved to Toledo when she married my father, but we used to visit my grandparents and spend holidays here.'

Carlos rarely spoke about his mother. Betsy found she was holding her breath, hoping he would open up more. 'What happened to her?'

A shadow crossed his face. 'She died suddenly from an undiagnosed medical condition. Both my grandparents outlived their daughter. Then the cottage was put up for sale by my uncle, who had inherited it, and I bought it to use as a bolthole.'

'Another bachelor pad like your penthouse in Madrid?' Betsy suggested.

'Apart from my sister, you are the only woman I've ever brought here.'

Carlos took off his sunglasses, and the gleam in his gold-flecked gaze made Betsy's heart-rate quicken.

'There's just us here. No staff. A woman from the village keeps an eye on the place and stocks the fridge when I tell her I'm coming.' He gave a disarming grin. 'I'll admit I can't cook, but there are several good restaurants locally.'

'I'm happy to cook. You used to like the meals I prepared for you when I was your housekeeper.'

'It wasn't just the meals you served that I liked, *querida*.'

She felt herself blush. Carlos's voice was like molten honey. 'Are you flirting with me?' she asked.

'Absolutely. I'm flirting with my wife on our honeymoon.' He picked up their bags, which he'd brought in from the car, and made for the stairs. 'I'll show you the rest of the house.'

Upstairs there were three smallish bedrooms and a couple of bathrooms. Carlos pushed open the door to the larger room. 'This is the master suite, where I usually sleep.' He set her bag down on the landing. 'Like I said, we're completely alone, and it's not necessary for us to share a bedroom. You can decide which room you want,' he said casually.

She bit her lip. 'This is our honeymoon…but you seem to be saying that we should sleep separately.' Frustration and hurt made her voice ragged. 'You blow hot and cold, and I don't know what you want from me.'

'I want you to feel you have choices, because so far I have given you none.' His jaw clenched. 'I forced you into marriage *and* into my bed.' He held his finger lightly against her lips when she tried to say something. 'I scared you. Why else would you have put that damn bolster between us? I would like you to be my wife in every sense. The truth is that I've kept away from you because I can't trust myself. You are beautiful, and sexy, and you drive me insane,' he said thickly. 'But I will respect your wishes if you choose a separate room.'

The band that had lashed around Betsy's heart when Carlos had returned to Spain two years ago unravelled. If sex was all he would give her then she would accept.

Passion without emotion was not perfect, but it was better than nothing. And Carlos wanted her as badly as she wanted him. She could see the restraint he was imposing on himself in the tense line of his jaw.

She picked up her holdall and walked through the door he had opened. 'I choose this room.' There was a hint of challenge in the tilt of her chin, and she held his brilliant gaze when he followed her into the master bedroom and closed the door, leaning his back against it. 'I choose you, Carlos.'

'Come here and take me, then, *mi belleza*,' he growled, in a voice so deep and dark it rolled through her.

Gone was the careless playboy—a reputation he had deliberately cultivated, Betsy realised. Now hunger sharpened his features, so that his skin was drawn tightly over his sculpted cheekbones. She took a step towards him and he levered himself away from the door and moved to stand in front of her. He was so close that she could see the faint grooves on either side of his mouth and hear the unevenness of his breaths.

Outside, dusk was falling, and the room was filled with soft shadows. Time slowed as he lowered his head and angled his mouth over hers. The first brush of his lips was gently evocative…a kiss of sweet delight as he eased her lips apart and sipped from her. His tenderness was unexpected, and she felt the press of tears behind her eyes.

Then he increased the pressure a fraction, and the kiss became a sensual feast, exquisitely erotic. He tasted her, coaxing a response from her, until suddenly his restraint snapped and he groaned and hauled her into his arms, deepening the kiss with the fierce passion that Betsy craved.

When at last he lifted his head, she stared into eyes that were molten gold and glazed with desire. 'I have a confession to make,' he said thickly. 'I instructed the maid not to pack your pyjamas.'

She smiled against his lips. 'How will I keep warm in the night?'

'I'll warm you with my body.' He trailed kisses down her throat, and then lower to the swell of her breasts. 'Shall I demonstrate?'

His hands were busy untying the straps of her sundress. He tugged the dress down to her waist and made an approving sound when he discovered that she was braless.

Her breasts felt heavy, the nipples taut and expectant as he kissed his way down her body and closed his mouth around one peak while he rolled its twin between his fingers. The pleasure he evoked with his simultaneous caresses sent an arrow of need to the core of her femininity.

Somehow her dress was on the floor, and his hand roamed over her bottom before he eased the panel of her knickers aside and rubbed his finger over her moist opening.

Her body was ready for him and her hands moved feverishly, tugging the buttons on his shirt open and pushing the material over his broad shoulders. He was

a work of art, and she gloried in the firmness of his ab-
dominal muscles. When she laid her palms flat on his
chest she felt the uneven thud of his heart, and when
she followed the arrowing of black hair down to the
waistband of his jeans and slid his zip down he muttered something in Spanish.

'I need you now.'

The admission was raw, ravenous, and the feral
gleam in his eyes sent a shiver of anticipation through
her. He shrugged out of the rest of his clothes with
haste rather than grace, and his impatience snagged
her emotions. She cupped his rough jaw between her
palms and pulled his mouth down onto hers, kissing
him with joy in her heart.

She *hadn't* imagined that their passion two years
ago had been out of the ordinary. Afterwards, she had
been ashamed of herself for falling into bed with him
so easily. But he was as irresistible now as he had been
then, and their mutual desire was blazing out of control.

He lifted her up and she wrapped her legs around
his hips as he carried her over to the bed. When he
laid her down and stretched out on top of her, she felt
the powerful muscles and sinews of his thighs, and the
hard length of his arousal jabbing her belly. He tugged
her panties off and skimmed his hand over the dusting
of caramel curls between her legs, parting her so that
he could slide one finger, two, into her molten heat.

She caught her breath as he began to move his hand.
'I want you…'

'*Sí*, I know, *querida*.'

'No, I want *you*.' Nothing but his full possession would ease the ache inside her.

He cursed softly. 'The condoms are in my jeans.' He started to move away from her, but she curled her arms around his neck.

'I asked the doctor who sees Sebastian when he's ill to give me a prescription for the pill.' She flushed. 'It seemed a good idea at the time.'

Carlos gave her a sexy smile and pulled her beneath him. 'So there is no reason not to do this?' he murmured, and he positioned himself over her so that the blunt tip of his erection nudged her opening. His eyes locked with hers as he pressed forward and eased his hard length into her slowly, so slowly, claiming her inch by exquisite inch.

It was better than she remembered. When she had given her virginity to him there had been slight discomfort, but now there was pure bliss as he pushed deeper and her internal muscles stretched to accommodate him. She lifted her hips towards him and splayed her fingers over his taut buttocks, drawing him deeper still so that he filled her.

'Ah, *querida*…' he said roughly, his lips against her throat.

And then his kissed her mouth, slow and sweet, and then hot and hungry as his body began to move within her. Each thrust was more satisfying than the one before, harder, faster, creating an erotic friction that drove her higher.

He supported his weight on his elbows and lengthened each rhythmic stroke. Dimly, Betsy was aware of the sound of her panting breaths…*his*. They moved together as one in the dance of lovers. She heard her blood pounding in her ears as it coursed through her veins, hotter, wilder. In his arms she became a wanton creature, tracing her hands boldly over his body so that he groaned.

'Now, *mi belleza*.'

'Yes.'

She quivered as he held her at the edge. His jaw was rigid, his eyes narrowed, and she felt the tension that gripped his big body. And then he thrust again, and she shattered around him, her internal muscles clenching and releasing and sending ripples of pleasure radiating from her core. He climaxed seconds after her, and his hoarse cry wrapped around her heart and lingered there long after their breathing had slowed.

He kissed the tears that clung to her eyelashes and rolled off her, drawing her against his side. *'Dios!'* His big chest rose and fell. 'I meant to take things slowly.' His voice was harsh with self-recrimination. 'Did I hurt you?'

'No. That was…' She was lost for words to describe the rapture of making love with him.

'Amazing,' he finished for her.

Betsy felt him smile against her brow as he kissed her hair, and it was that little affectionate gesture which delighted her the most. But she reminded herself to guard her foolish heart against falling for her enigmatic husband…

CHAPTER ELEVEN

'I SEEM TO remember you promised me a sightseeing trip today,' Betsy said lightly.

Carlos was propped on an elbow, lying on the blanket that they had spread out on the sand. His eyes roamed over her tiny silver bikini top. Since they had come to Casita Viola ten days ago he had tested the weight of her firm breasts countless times and felt the thrust of her nipples against his tongue. But, however many times he had her, he wanted her again and again.

'I am enjoying the sight of you, *querida*. Although the view would be even better if you took your top off,' he murmured, stretching out his hand and tugging at the ties.

She laughed and evaded his fingers. 'You're insatiable.'

'Is that a complaint?'

Beneath his teasing, he was serious. He was sure that Betsy enjoyed their lovemaking as much as he did, but he found his desire for her was limitless. In a distant corner of his mind an alarm bell rang, but he ignored it and bent his head to claim her mouth in a lingering kiss.

He was in control, he assured himself. But he was at Casita Viola, the place he loved more than anywhere in the world, with his beautiful, sexy wife, and there was no harm in letting his guard down a little.

When he slipped his hand between Betsy's soft thighs, she pushed against his chest. 'Food,' she muttered. 'I'm going to make lunch, and afterwards we will have a siesta.'

'I'll hold you to that promise, *querida*. And later I'll keep mine and take you to Palma. It's a beautiful city to explore. We won't have any time for sightseeing after Sebastian arrives tomorrow.'

'I can't wait to see him. I've missed him.' Betsy grinned and jumped up from the blanket. 'Although you *have* kept me entertained.'

Carlos watched her walk up the cliff steps to the house, admiring her pert derriere, barely covered by tiny denim shorts. The idea of a honeymoon had been a stroke of genius, he congratulated himself. These past days had been a revelation, and he and Betsy had both been more relaxed without the strain that their relationship had been under before.

Carlos acknowledged that the main reason for his good mood was the fact that he was getting great sex regularly. As he'd suspected, he and Betsy were highly sexually compatible. Not only that, he liked being with her. She was good company, witty and funny, and he was genuinely interested in her.

He was aware that while he'd expected Betsy to leave her old life and her friends in Dorset and move to

Spain, he had not had to make *any* sacrifices. Of course he'd had to give up his freedom, but he didn't miss his playboy lifestyle when he had a far more meaningful life as a father. And besides, he hadn't looked at another woman for longer than he cared to recall. Making Betsy happy had become his mission. Having a contented wife made life a lot easier than having her unhappy with their marriage arrangement, he reasoned.

After a swim in the sea, Carlos made his way back to the house and found Betsy carrying a bowl of salad outside to the terrace, where she had set the table for lunch.

'Can you bring the wine from the kitchen?' she called to him.

He uncorked the bottle of red wine that had been produced at a local vineyard before he followed her outside.

'While I was looking for a clean tablecloth I found some photo albums with pictures of you when you were younger,' Betsy said, indicating the albums on the table. 'Do you mind if I look through them after lunch?'

'Help yourself.'

They ate fresh prawns that Carlos had bought from a local fisherman, and then carried their wine glasses over to a corner of the garden shaded by a pergola, where vivid pink bougainvillea grew in abundance.

'Is that you?' Betsy asked, pointing to a photo of a small boy holding a tennis racket that was almost as big as him.

'I must have been about three years old then. My mother introduced me to tennis at an early age.' Carlos pointed to another photo. 'I was eight in this one, and I'd just won an under-twelves regional championship. My mother realised that I had talent, and she hired José Vidal, who had been her tennis coach when she played professionally, to work with me.'

'I didn't realise that your mother was a tennis player.'

'She was runner-up in the Spanish and French championships, and she played in London on a wild card and got to the quarter-finals. It was her dream to win the BITC, but she retired from the game to focus on her family.'

'You must have been close to her with your shared love of tennis,' Betsy said softly. She looked at a photo of Carlos laughing with his father. 'It looks as though you had a strong bond with your dad, too.'

'We were close once.' Guilt snaked through Carlos. 'Everything changed when my mother died.'

He could see that Betsy was curious, but he wasn't about to tell her that he had his mother's blood on his hands, and that was why his father had turned against him. If he admitted what he had done he was certain he would see disgust in Betsy's eyes.

With a jolt of shock, Carlos realised that her opinion of him mattered.

'Who is this?' she asked, indicating a picture of a man standing next to a teenage Carlos.

'That's my coach, José. When I was fifteen, I was offered funding on the condition that I moved to Barcelona to train. My father ran a business in Toledo, and couldn't uproot my sister, so I left home and lodged with José and his wife.'

'You had recently lost your mother, hadn't you? It must have been hard to leave your father and sister, and they must have missed you.'

'My father wanted me to go.'

In his mind, Carlos heard Roderigo Segarra's voice. *'Don't let your mother's death be in vain. Go and learn to be a champion for her sake. It's the least you can do to honour her memory.'*

But Carlos had been prepared to give up his pursuit of the dream that had torn his family apart. *'I'll stay, Papà, and learn to be a baker so that I can take over the shop, like you hoped I would.'*

Roderigo had actually looked horrified at the prospect. *'My hopes died with your mother,'* he'd said bitterly. *'I don't want you to stay here.'*

They had been devastating words to a fifteen-year-old boy, and twenty years later his father's rejection still scraped a raw place on Carlos's heart.

'José Vidal was my coach for ten years,' he told Betsy. 'He became a father figure to me, and I trusted him. I was certain that with his support I would become the greatest tennis champion. By my early twenties I was ranked number three in the world and had already won four world titles.'

He lifted his glass to his lips and drank some wine.

'I'll admit that fame and glory went to my head.' His laugh was self-derisive. 'I endorsed several big sports brands and got paid a fortune for using a certain tennis racket or modelling a particular range of sportswear. I had money, and beautiful women flocked around me. Training took second place to living the good life. But everything changed when I got very drunk one night and fell down a flight of steps. My shoulder was broken in three places and there was significant muscle and ligament damage. The surgeon was doubtful that I would play tennis at competition level again.'

Betsy looked shocked. 'I had no idea. You must have felt devastated, believing that your career could be over.'

It had been a bleak time in his life, and Carlos rarely allowed himself to dwell on it. Like other dark events in his past, he compartmentalised the memories and buried them deep inside him. He had no idea why he was spilling his guts to Betsy.

'More devastating than my injuries was the attitude of my coach. José came to visit me in hospital and told me that he would no longer oversee my training. He'd read the medical reports and didn't believe I would ever recover properly and regain my tennis ranking. As far as he was concerned I wouldn't be a champion and earn the big money, so he dropped me in favour of another rising tennis star.'

'That's awful.'

There was a sympathy in Betsy's voice that Carlos told himself he neither wanted nor deserved.

'That's life,' he said harshly. 'When I watched José walk out of that hospital room, I vowed two things. The first was that I would be a champion without his

help, and the second was that I would never trust anyone again.'

Carlos stared at another photo. It was of him, his
parents and his sister, who had been only ten at the
time. It was the last picture of his family before his
mother had died. Thinking about her made his heart
grow heavy. His *madre* would have loved Sebastian,
and her other grandson Miguel. But her life had been
cruelly cut short—by *him*.

Carlos's jaw clenched. He did not deserve a family
after he'd destroyed the one he had been born into. He
hadn't planned to have a child, but fate had intervened
and given him a son he adored. He had a wife too, although he hadn't expected to marry.

He had married Betsy so that he could claim his
son, he reminded himself. But deep down he knew that
hadn't been the only reason.

He forced his mind away from the past, aware that
Betsy was looking at him with a concerned expression
on her face. 'You mentioned a siesta,' he murmured.

'Carlos…' She lifted a hand and let it fall helplessly.
'You told me that there are things I don't understand.
But how *can* I understand, or try to help you, if you
don't talk to me?'

'Help me?' He shook his head. 'All the talking in
the world won't make any difference. There is nothing you can do.'

She tilted her chin. 'Try me.'

He remembered how she had defended him against
his father's criticism, and was almost tempted to re-

veal the dark secret that festered inside him. But shame stopped him.

The silence stretched between them until Betsy gave a soft sigh and stood up. 'I need a shower before we go to Palma.'

Carlos told himself he wouldn't follow her. But when Betsy walked into the house he felt as if she had taken the sunshine with her and coldness seeped into his bones.

He did not need her. That was a ridiculous idea, he assured himself. But somehow he was standing in the bedroom and staring at her silver bikini that she'd left on the floor outside the bathroom door.

Carlos stripped off his swim shorts and stepped into the steamy shower cubicle. He paused for a moment, watching the water cascade over Betsy's gorgeous curves, and then moved to stand behind her. He slid his arms around her and cupped her breasts in his hands, pulling her against him so that her bottom was pressing on his erection.

'I have a surprise for you when we go back to Fortaleza Aguila,' he murmured in her ear.

She wriggled out of his arms and turned to face him. 'What is it?'

'It won't be a surprise if I tell you.'

He inhaled sharply when she dropped to her knees in front of him. Water streamed over her face and hair as she looked up at him, and her smile was like a sunbeam lighting the darkness in his heart.

'Maybe I can persuade you to tell me,' she said softly.

And then she put her mouth on him, and he could not control the shudders that racked him when she moved her tongue along his hard length.

That alarm bell in his mind rang again. Control was everything to Carlos, and losing control was a weakness he could not contemplate. For twenty years he had not allowed anything to touch him deeply enough so that he cared.

He told himself that he did not care about Betsy, beyond the fact that she was the mother of his son. The passion they shared was just a bonus in their marriage, and he had no doubt that in time his physical infatuation with her would settle to something less needy that he could control.

But in the meantime he threaded his fingers into her hair as he fell back against the wall of the shower cubicle and lost control spectacularly.

'Do you want to see your surprise?' Carlos asked Betsy as she walked down the stairs at Fortaleza Aguila. They had arrived at the house twenty minutes ago and she'd just carried Sebastian up to the nursery.

'I'm sure he has grown taller,' Ginette had said fondly as she'd watched the toddler charge over to his toy box. 'Did you and Carlos have a relaxing holiday?'

Betsy had felt herself blush as she'd thought of the amount of mind-blowing sex they'd had. Their honeymoon had been the most exhilarating few weeks of her life. But it wasn't only physically that her relationship with Carlos had developed. They had grown closer in so many other ways and had talked for hours.

The time they had spent together in Mallorca had reminded her of when she had been his housekeeper in London and cooked dinner for them every evening. Carlos had needed to unwind after his heavy training sessions or playing matches when the tournament had begun. Often they had watched a film together, or read, and they'd both tried to ignore the sexual chemistry that had simmered between them until that last night, when it had exploded into passion.

At Casita Viola, Betsy had cooked Carlos's favourite meals and taken pleasure in his enjoyment of the food she'd prepared. When Ginette had brought Sebastian to Mallorca and then returned to Toledo, Betsy had loved the fact that they were a little family. She'd been happy, pottering about the cottage or taking Sebastian to the beach. And at night, when their son had been tucked up in his cot, Carlos had brought her body to quivering life with his caresses and she had acknowledged that she was halfway to being in love with him.

Her heart gave a familiar flip as she walked across the hall towards him. Sun-bleached jeans hugged his lean hips, and a black tee shirt moulded his magnificent chest.

'Is my surprise in your study?' she asked.

She was puzzled when he opened the door and ushered her into the room.

'Oh!'

She stopped dead and looked around in amazement.

The study had been transformed into an art studio. An easel stood next to the window, and there was a long workbench and storage drawers beneath it, a table with her sketchbook and pencils, and at one end of the room a big leather sofa.

'The sofa is for me, when I come and visit you in your studio,' Carlos told her with a grin.

'But you need your study. You often work from home.'

'I've relocated to another room. Your friend Hector said that this was the best room for natural light coming through the window.'

She stared at him. 'You asked Hector?'

'While we were in Mallorca I phoned the art supplies shop and spoke to him. He was very helpful, advising me on what equipment you would need. I thought you might like to invite Hector and his girlfriend to dinner one evening. You have met my friends—it's about time I got to know yours,' Carlos said.

She swallowed the lump in her throat. 'I can't believe you've done such a lovely thing for me. I've always wanted a proper studio.'

'I'm glad you like it. It's important to me that we make a success of our marriage, *querida*.'

'It is?' Tremulous hope filled her.

'Of course. Sebastian deserves to have parents who are united.'

Betsy could not fault his reasoning. And her parents' love had turned to hatred. So why did she yearn for Carlos to see her as more than the mother of his child? Her pleasure in the studio was dimmed slightly, knowing that he believed it was his *duty* to keep her happy. When she was a child her parents had competed for who could buy her the most expensive birthday and Christmas presents, but all she'd really wanted was for them to love her instead of using her to argue over.

Carlos captured her chin and tilted her face up to his. 'You look sad. Did I forget something for the studio?'

'No, it's perfect.' She sternly told herself to stop wishing for the moon and smiled at him. 'Thank you.'

'I think we should try out the sofa.' He drew her into his arms and nuzzled the sensitive spot behind her ear. 'I had a lock fitted on the door so that you won't be disturbed when you are working.'

'I'm not working now...'

Her breath hitched in her throat when he slipped his hand beneath her tee shirt and cupped a breast, dragging his thumb across its tender peak.

'That's why I locked the door,' he said thickly, and he dropped down on the sofa and pulled her onto his lap.

Desire gleamed golden bright in his eyes and Betsy melted instantly, as she always did when her handsome husband made love to her. But she could not ignore the whispered warning in her head.

If his passion for her faded in the future, would he still be committed to their marriage?

But Carlos threaded his fingers through her hair with a tenderness that lit a spark of hope inside her, and when he claimed her mouth she pushed her doubts away and sank into his kiss.

* * *

The days slipped into weeks, and the fiercely hot temperature so characteristic of Toledo in midsummer dropped a few degrees to become pleasantly warm in early autumn.

Betsy put down her brush and stepped back from the easel to study her latest animal portrait with a critical eye. The horse she was painting was owned by Carlos's close friend Sergio and his wife Martina. The couple often came to dinner and Betsy had discovered that she and Martina, who owned a riding stables, shared a love of animals. Also, Martina's sister Mia had a daughter the same age as Sebastian, and had invited Betsy to a mother and baby group.

It helped that she was picking up more Spanish words, so that she was able to chat to the other mothers in the group, and Sebastian loved playing with other children.

She and Carlos had also met Hector and his girlfriend for dinner and the two men had got on well. Now that she had a social life with new friends, and her pet portrait business was doing so well that she had a waiting list of clients, Betsy felt more settled.

She moved closer to the window overlooking the garden and watched Carlos playing with their son. He had already introduced Sebastian to a child-sized tennis racket and spongy balls. At nearly eighteen months old, the toddler showed amazing hand-eye coordination.

'Do you hope Sebastian will be a tennis champion?' Betsy had asked Carlos once.

'I'll support him in whatever he chooses to do,' Carlos had replied, with an odd note in his voice.

She remembered he'd said that his father had not been proud of his sporting success, but her attempts to get Carlos to open up about his strained relationship with Roderigo had been politely but firmly rebuffed.

Betsy gave a soft sigh. To other people her marriage must seem perfect. And it almost was. She and Carlos got on brilliantly, and they spent a lot of time together because he was often at home now. He'd cut down on his business trips, saying that he wanted to be with Sebastian as much as possible.

She would always feel guilty that she'd stolen the first fifteen months of his son's life from him, but Carlos had said that they had both made mistakes and it was time to put the past behind them and move on.

As for the physical side of their marriage—it got better and better. There was no longer a bolster down the centre of the bed, and they made love most nights. The sofa in her art studio had proved to be very useful too… Heat stained Betsy's face as she recalled how Carlos had bent her over the leather arm while he stood behind her and eased his erection between her thighs.

He took her apart every time he made love to her, but he never lost control with complete abandon the way he'd done at the cottage. She longed to shatter his restraint, but he seemed determined not to allow it to happen, and sex had become something of a battle of wills which Betsy always lost.

Yes, her life was very nearly perfect—especially now there was a new member of their family. She looked over at the fluffy bundle of mischief who was curled up in a dog basket.

'He's half miniature poodle and the other half is anyone's guess,' Carlos had said a few weeks ago when he'd carried the small, apricot-coloured dog into the house and placed him in Betsy's arms. 'The staff at the dog rescue centre think he's about a year old, and he's good around children. His previous owner died, which is why he is up for adoption.' Carlos had hesitated when Betsy had looked stunned. 'I thought you would like him.'

'He's the most beautiful dog in the world,' she'd said in a choked voice when she'd been able to speak. 'Are you sure we can keep him?' She'd been afraid to get her hopes up.

'He's yours, *querida*,' Carlos had told her gruffly. 'The name on his collar is Chico, but I guess you can choose a different name for him.'

Now, Betsy walked across her studio and opened the door. 'Come, Chico!' The little dog was instantly at her feet, tail wagging.

Chico's unconditional love helped to ease the ache in her heart but did not erase it. She told herself she was greedy to want more than she had. A healthy son, a beautiful home and an attentive and charming husband. Her marriage exceeded all her expectations.

But she was in love with Carlos—deeply, desperately in love with him.

It wasn't the gifts he'd given her—although her studio and her dog brought her so much joy, and she appreciated the jewellery and flowers he often surprised her with. She loved him because he was a wonderful father to Sebastian. And he took an interest in her art and treated her as if she mattered to him.

But she knew he only did those things because she was the mother of his child, and the stark truth was that if she hadn't fallen pregnant two years ago, Carlos would never have returned to England to find her.

The butler met Betsy in the entrance hall when she stepped out of her studio. '*Un paquete* is here for you,' Eduardo said haltingly as he handed her a padded envelope.

It had an English postmark and Betsy was curious as she opened the envelope and found another parcel. Inside this was a slim box, and when she lifted the lid she gasped at the sight of a row of diamonds sparkling on a black velvet cushion. It was known as a tennis bracelet—a single row of diamonds on a gold chain.

Also in the box was a card with her name on, and a message scrawled in a bold hand.

Mi querida Betsy,
   Perhaps you will wear this bracelet and think of me.
   Call me if you would like to meet me again.

I hope to hear from you soon.
Carlos.

At the bottom of the card was a phone number.

Carlos *hadn't* abandoned her after they'd spent the night together. He *had* wanted to see her again.

Betsy's hands shook as she read the note which had been inside the envelope. It was from her Aunt Alice's son, the one who had inherited the house in London when Alice died.

Betsy,
I recently found this parcel addressed to you while I was clearing out the unit where my mother's personal belongings were stored when the house was sold. I remembered that it arrived after you moved away.

Hope it wasn't important.
Lee

On the back of the envelope was the sender's name and address. *Bradley Miller.* Of course! Betsy remembered that Alice's son's full name was Bradley, but he always used the abbreviation Lee. He must have signed for the delivery as B. Miller, exactly as the courier had reported to Carlos.

The parcel containing the bracelet *was* important. It changed everything.

CHAPTER TWELVE

WAS SHE CRAZY? Probably, Betsy answered herself. She hugged her arms around herself as nerves threatened to overwhelm her. She was about to take the biggest gamble of her life, and if it failed she would be looking into the abyss.

But it wouldn't fail, she tried to assure herself. When she'd opened the parcel earlier in the day and discovered the bracelet Carlos had sent her two years ago, she had been convinced it was proof that he had felt something for her. She hadn't been just a casual fling as he'd told the journalist.

If only she had been at the house in London and read his note when it had been delivered. She would have called him and told him she was pregnant. It was bittersweet to realise that things could have been so different. Carlos would have met his son when he was born instead of fifteen months later.

She couldn't give him back the time he'd missed with Sebastian. But at least he would know now that she hadn't lied when she'd denied receiving the parcel. She had always been honest with him, and it was only right that she should be honest about her feelings for him now.

'Are we celebrating something?'

Carlo's deep voice was indulgent as he strolled across the terrace. Betsy had asked the staff to set up a table and two chairs beside the pool. She gave a tense glance at the snowy white cloth, silver cutlery and long-stemmed glasses to check that everything was perfect. An arrangement of white roses in the centre of the table gave off a heady perfume. Her fingers were unsteady as she lit the candles before she turned to face him. She smoothed her hand nervously down the black silk sheath dress that fitted her like a second skin.

'I thought it would be nice to dress up for dinner,' she said huskily. Carlos looked mouthwatering in fitted black trousers and a soft cream shirt unbuttoned at the throat. 'I've been wearing my painting shirt all day while I finished Sergio and Martina's picture.'

'You look amazing in that dress,' he murmured as he stood in front of her. The dress had a halter neck and Carlos brushed his lips over one bare shoulder. 'I hope you haven't planned a dinner with many courses, because I'm ready for dessert now, *mi belleza*.'

Her heart lurched as her awareness of him, as always, collided with her nerves. He smelled divine. The evocative scent of his sandalwood cologne teased her senses and suddenly she felt shy—which was ridiculous when he had seen every inch of her body, and stared into her eyes and glimpsed her soul each time she'd climaxed beneath him.

'Let's sit down,' she said jerkily.

His gaze sharpened on her hot face, but he said nothing as he pulled out her chair and waited for her to be seated before he moved around the table and sat down. The first course of gazpacho, a traditional Spanish cold soup, was already in bowls in front of them.

Betsy lifted the cover from her bowl and reached for the bottle of red wine that she'd asked the butler to uncork and leave open to breathe. As she filled Carlos's glass the diamond bracelet on her wrist sparkled in the candlelight. He stared at the bracelet and then at her.

'My aunt's son found the package that you sent to the house in London and posted it on to me. I remember I asked you once what a tennis bracelet was. Now I know.' She turned her wrist and the diamonds glittered. 'I'm two years too late, but it's beautiful. Thank you.'

He leaned back in his chair. 'So you really didn't receive the gift I sent you when I returned to Spain?'

She shook her head. 'If I'd had your phone number I would have called you. Fate is capricious,' she murmured. 'Things would have been different if I had known that you wanted to see me again.'

'In what way different?'

'I assume we would have been together when Sebastian was born, and there would not have been all these misunderstandings between us.'

He nodded. 'It's true. I would have married you

when I learned of your pregnancy to ensure that my child was legitimate at his birth.'

Carlos's matter-of-fact statement sent a ripple of unease through Betsy. 'But my pregnancy wouldn't have been the only reason you'd have married me, would it?'

His brows drew together. 'What do you mean?'

She put down her spoon, her soup untouched, and lifted her arm to look at the diamond bracelet. 'You sent me a beautiful gift and said you wanted to see me again. That means a lot to me.' Her voice shook. 'I love the bracelet…and I love you, Carlos. I fell in love with you two years ago, and I think… I hope…you feel the same way about me.'

Something flared in his eyes, but was gone before she could assimilate what it was she had seen. And maybe she'd imagined it. His face was a beautiful sculpted mask that revealed no emotion, and his silence seemed faintly stunned, pressing against Betsy's ears. Her stomach cramped with nervous tension at the creeping realisation that she might have gotten things horribly wrong.

'I don't share your feelings,' he said abruptly.

She bit down on her lip hard and tasted blood in her mouth. 'So if I hadn't fallen pregnant, if we hadn't had Sebastian, where would our relationship have been?' Ice formed around her heart. 'Or are you saying that we wouldn't have had a relationship? Even though you must have felt *something* for me to have sent the bracelet?'

He dropped his gaze from hers. 'That wasn't the first time I'd given a bracelet as a gift.'

Understanding dawned, and she would have sworn she actually heard her heart shatter. 'You used to send bracelets to women when you wanted to have an affair with them. It was your calling card, and I was just one in a long line of casual flings like you told that journalist, wasn't I?'

'You didn't want high emotion and drama,' Carlos reminded her, almost aggressively. 'Your parents' volatile relationship ruined your childhood. You don't want that for Sebastian, and nor do I.' He raked his hair off his brow. 'What we have is good—solid. A marriage based on reason and common sense and a desire to do the best for our son.'

'Is that really all our marriage is to you?' She had built castles in the air and now they were tumbling down. 'Our honeymoon felt like more than common sense.'

He looked away from her. 'I needed to break the deadlock between us.'

'And so you seduced me?'

'If you remember, *querida*, you seduced *me*,' he said softly.

She had made it so easy for him, Betsy thought bleakly. He had spun his sensual web and she'd walked straight into it.

'The passion we share is unique,' he said. 'I have never wanted any woman the way I want you.'

'Is that supposed to make me feel better? That I'm a good lay?'

'You know that's not what I meant.' He picked up his wine glass and drained it in a couple of gulps. 'I have never wanted to fall in love. I told you when I asked you to marry me that we wouldn't have a fairy tale romance.' He gave her a frustrated look. 'I'm not cut out for love.'

'You love Sebastian.'

He lifted his shoulders. 'That's different. I had no choice. The moment I held my son I was overwhelmed with love for him.'

'But you don't love me,' she said quietly.

She seemed to have spent most of her life being quiet, not making a fuss so that then maybe everything would be all right and the shouting would stop. She wanted to curl up in a ball and pull the duvet over her head, like she'd done as a child to block out her parents' angry voices. Now she wanted to block out the pity she'd heard in Carlos's voice. *Pity*.

She felt sick. Her throat burned with the tears that she was trying to swallow because she couldn't let herself break down in front of him.

He scraped back his chair and stood up. 'You don't want me to love you. Really you don't, *querida*. I am no good at it.'

Beneath his savage voice there was a rawness that startled Betsy.

'*I'm* no good,' Carlos told her grimly.

And then he walked away, leaving her alone with her heart in a thousand pieces.

How long she sat there she did not know. The butler came with the main course and she sent him back to the kitchen with her apologies to the cook. Betsy did not think she would ever want to eat again, or smile, or paint. Life had been drained of joy.

If only she had been content with what she had instead of wanting more. She had put Carlos under pressure to admit how he felt about her and his answer had ripped her heart out. Now that she had revealed her emotions they would not be able to return to how they had been.

The thought of facing him again made her insides squirm. She couldn't share a bed with him and make love with him, knowing that for him it was just sex. How could she stay with him now she knew that he would never love her as she loved him?

She stood up and blew out the flames on the candles that had burnt down almost to nothing. A muscle in her leg twinged and she realised that she had been sitting in the same position for too long. Sleep would be impossible, and she didn't even know where she would go to bed.

Filled with restlessness, she walked into the pool house and changed into her one-piece costume before she headed back to the pool. The underwater lights had come on and she dived into the water and started to swim, length after length, punishing herself for wanting the one thing she could not have. Her husband's heart.

He had hurt her. He'd seen the evidence in the way her mouth had crumpled and her eyes had shimmered over-bright in the candlelight.

But what else could he have done? Carlos asked

himself as guilt jagged through him. He couldn't have lied and made false promises. Betsy deserved better than that. She deserved his honesty. She was so honest herself, and fierce and brave and loving. He saw her generous nature every day as she showered their son with love. Betsy had a big heart and a deep well of kindness. She cared for her friends and she adored the little dog which was utterly devoted to her. She was charming to the staff and she took Sebastian to visit his grandfather daily.

And she loved him.

Carlos cursed as he strode through the house with no idea of where he was headed. The bottom of a whisky bottle was tempting. But he couldn't hide from his demons any longer. He couldn't keep running. Betsy *loved* him. But she wouldn't if she knew what he had done. He didn't deserve her love.

But he wanted it.

His breath left him on a groan and he stumbled and leaned against the wall, feeling as if he'd been winded. Feeling as if his heart was being squeezed in a vice. This was why he had spent his adult life burying his emotions. Love hurt. It was killing him to know that he had hurt Betsy.

This was the truth of him, Carlos thought savagely. He destroyed everything that was good.

A memory that he had spent twenty years trying to eradicate by pushing his body to the extreme of its physical capability slid like a poisonous serpent into his mind. His mother lying slumped on the tennis court while he cradled her in his arms, feeling helpless as the life left her body on a shuddering final breath. He'd sprinted over to where he'd left his bag and grabbed his phone, but even as he'd called the emergency services he'd known it was too late.

He remembered how tears had streamed down his father's face. 'You knew your mother felt unwell with a headache, but still you nagged her to be your practice partner. All you care about is tennis and the glory of winning. Now your mother has paid the price for your ambition with her life. Never forget that, Carlos.'

He looked around and discovered that his feet had brought him to the annexe of the house. He hammered on the door of his father's suite and the nurse let him in. He strode into his father's bedroom. Roderigo rarely left his bed these days, and his bony hand pressed the control to bring him up into a sitting position.

'Why didn't you come to watch me play in the London final? I wanted you to be there.' The words burst out of Carlos. 'I won it for *her*. I thought you would be proud of me at last.' The ache in his chest expanded. 'I hoped you would forgive me, Papà.'

'I couldn't bring myself to go,' his father rasped. 'It had been your mother's dream to win the ladies' tournament there.' He sighed. 'She could have done it. She was a great player, and her coach said she had the potential to be a world champion. But I stopped her from pursuing her dream. I resented the hours of training she put in, and the weeks and months she spent away on the tennis tours. I put pressure on her to start a family. I told her I wanted a child—a son who would one day take over the bakery from me as I had done when my father retired. But motherhood meant the end of her tennis career.'

Carlos stared at his father. 'Are you saying that Mamà did not want me?'

'She wanted you,' Roderigo said softly. 'Your mother adored you and Graciela. She never regretted choosing to be a mother. But as you grew up, and it became apparent that you had inherited her talent for tennis, I realised how much she had missed playing competitively. She lived her dream through you, and I resented you because your success reminded me of the career she might have had if my selfishness hadn't denied her the chance to chase her dream.'

Carlos swallowed. 'You sent me away to live in Barcelona. You blamed me for her death and you were right. I killed her.'

'I regret what I said. I was in shock. I didn't really blame you. I didn't realise that you had remembered it for all these years.'

'It wasn't something I was likely to forget,' Carlos said curtly.

'Forgive me.' A tear slid down Roderigo's papery cheek. 'Your mother had died and it was too late for me tell her that I was sorry, that I wished I'd encouraged her tennis career. I couldn't go to watch you in London because *she* should have played there and I felt so guilty. I sent you to live with your coach because I was determined to give you the chance that I had taken away from you mother. You are a great champion and she would have been proud of you…as I am proud of you, *mi hijo*.'

'Papà…' Carlos sat on the bed and clasped his father's hand.

'You have a beautiful wife and son. Don't make the mistakes I made.' Roderigo squeezed Carlos's fingers. 'Don't leave things unsaid and spend the rest of your life regretting it.'

Carlos's mind was reeling as he left the annexe and returned to the main house. The glass doors were open in the sitting room, and he frowned when he heard someone shouting. The room overlooked the pool terrace, and he saw the butler running across the tiles.

'La señora—se ha ahogada!'

Drowned!

Carlos tore down the steps from the house. As he raced across the terrace he saw a shape lying motionless next to the pool. His heart slammed against his ribs. In his mind he saw his mother, slumped on the tennis court.

'Betsy!'

His roar was that of a wounded animal. He dropped onto his knees beside her, relief pouring through him when she half sat up and coughed up water.

She groaned and clutched her leg. 'Cramp in my calf muscle,' she muttered. 'I was swimming and my leg seized up. I couldn't move. Luckily Eduardo saw me and managed to pull me out of the water.'

'It's all right, *querida*.' Carlos's hands were shaking as he gathered her close.

She tensed and pulled away from him. 'It's not all right,' she choked, 'and it never will be. I've ruined everything.'

Betsy would rather have walked over hot coals than for Carlos to lift her into his arms. But the pain in her calf muscle was so excruciating that walking was impossible, and she had no choice but to suffer him carrying her back to the house.

'You can put me down on the sofa. I'll be fine in a few minutes,' she muttered, her gaze fixed on his shirt collar rather than on his face.

He ignored her and strode across the hall and up the stairs, heading along the corridor towards their bedroom. They had separate bathrooms, but hers only had a shower. He carried her into his and sat her on a chair while he turned on the taps to fill the bath, adding a handful of bath crystals.

'Hot water will help the muscle to relax. Cramp in the gastrocnemius—that's the big muscle in your calf—is agony,' he explained. 'I was once carried off a tennis court halfway through a match that I was winning because of cramp.'

She suspected he was chatting normally to make her feel less embarrassed. *Some hope*, Betsy thought bleakly. His kindness made things so much worse.

She stared down at her feet so that he would not see the tears brimming in her eyes. 'The pain is going off a bit. I can manage now. Will you go and check on Sebastian?'

'Don't lock the door in case you need my help.'

When he had gone, she peeled off her swimsuit and climbed into the bath. It was deep and she sank into the water, flexing the calf muscle that now ached dully. Her mind replayed those terrifying minutes in the pool, when she'd literally been unable to move her leg. The pain had been so intense that she had panicked and swallowed a mouthful of pool water.

Tears slipped down her cheeks. She told herself they were a reaction to shock but knew she was lying to herself. There was a movement by the door, and through her tears she saw Carlos's blurred figure leaning against the frame.

'When I was fourteen I had the chance to become the youngest player to win an international boys' tournament, but I lost the final match,' he said heavily. 'I was furious and I lost my temper. I had a complete meltdown on the court and smashed my racket. I received an official reprimand from the umpire. In the car afterwards, my father told me that my behaviour had brought shame on the family. My mother was upset. When we got home, she said she had a headache. But I nagged her to come to the practice court and be my hitting partner.'

He pushed his hands into his pockets and kicked the door frame with his toe.

'I served a ball hard and it caught her on her shoulder. She fell to the ground. I was annoyed because I thought she was making a fuss. But she didn't move.'

Betsy held her breath as Carlos continued.

'I ran across to her and supported her head in my arms. I still thought she had been hurt by the tennis ball and she would get up in a minute. But she died. Right there in my arms, my mother died.'

'Oh, Carlos, I'm so sorry.'

His face twisted. 'It wasn't the tennis ball. She died of a brain aneurysm. The headache had been a warning sign. Someone called my father and he came to the tennis court, but he was too late. He sobbed like a child over my mother's body—and then he told me that I had killed her.'

'I don't believe that,' Betsy said urgently. 'The aneurysm could have ruptured at any time.'

He nodded. 'But I was convinced that my hot temper had resulted in my mother's death, and I vowed never to lose control of my emotions ever again. *Any* of my emotions,' he said roughly. 'For twenty years I never got angry, or sad, or wildly happy. I didn't allow myself to feel anything too deeply.'

The pain in his voice tore on her heart. 'Carlos…'

'And then I met you, Betsy Miller. You were my housekeeper and you assured me that I wouldn't notice you.'

He smiled ruefully, but the expression in his eyes made her heart lurch.

'I wanted you from that moment.'

'And after I had fallen into your bed like a ripe plum,

you decided you would have an affair with me.' The bubbles were rapidly disappearing, and she sank lower in the bathwater. 'If I had seen your note and met you in Spain I suppose you would have invited me to stay at your bachelor penthouse in Madrid, until you grew bored with a shy housekeeper and ditched me for a glamorous model.'

'That bathwater must be getting cold.'

He levered himself away from the door and, before Betsy realised his intention, leaned down and scooped her out of the bath.

'I'm making you wet,' she muttered as he held her against his chest and carried her into the bedroom. Being in his arms was torture, and she longed to press her lips to his rough jaw. When he sat her on the bed, she grabbed the towel he offered and wrapped it around herself.

'I planned to take you to Mallorca, to Casita Viola,' he said.

She stared at him. 'I thought you never invited your lovers to the cottage?'

'I didn't.'

He hesitated for a heartbeat, and Betsy had the crazy idea that he was unsure of himself.

'But you were different.'

Yet more tears filled her eyes. She wanted to believe him so badly, but he'd warned her not to believe in fairy tales. 'Carlos, please don't feel sorry for me. I shouldn't have said what I did at dinner.'

'You told me that you loved me.'

His voice was velvet-soft and she tried to steel herself against his tenderness. He was a nice guy, and he was trying to let her down gently.

'Do we have to have a post-mortem on how I made a fool of myself again?'

The mattress dipped as Carlos sat beside her and captured her chin, tilting her face up to his. Gold-flecked eyes searched her gaze. 'Did you mean it?'

She gave a little sigh. He was her world, and now she understood how he had been affected by his mother's death. He was afraid of strong emotions, and wary of love, but perhaps in time he would grow to care for her.

'I have never lied to you,' she said softly.

'*Santa Madre!*'

He closed his eyes briefly, and when he opened them again his expression stopped Betsy's heart in its tracks.

'I love you, *mi corazón...mi amor.*'

A tear slid down her cheek and he caught it on his thumb. 'Why are you shaking your head, *querida?* Don't you want me to love you?'

His voice was rough, uncertain, and her tears fell faster. 'I want your love so much, but I'm scared to believe you.'

'Why would I lie?'

His smile stole her breath and, impossibly, she saw that his lashes were damp.

'How could I not love you, Betsy? You stole my heart two years ago. But I had got used to feeling nothing. It was easier...safer. I couldn't hurt anyone if I didn't care about them.' His mouth twisted. 'And I couldn't be hurt if I didn't fall in love. I tried to deny how I felt about you, but when I saw you next to the pool tonight I thought—' he swallowed hard '—I feared I had lost you. And I had to face the fact that without you the world is grey, because you are my sunshine and I will love you for eternity.'

She fell into his arms, because it was the only place she wanted to be. His heart thundered beneath her hands as she tugged open his shirt buttons and pressed her face against his warm olive skin.

She could not quite believe that he was hers, but when she lifted her head the golden gleam in his eyes was love—pure and precious and all for her. With a soft cry of joy she curled her arms around his neck and pulled his head down. He claimed her mouth and kissed her fiercely, but with an innate tenderness that told her without words that his love was the lasting kind.

'I love you. And it will last, won't it?' she whispered as he unwrapped the towel from around her body and stripped off his clothes before stretching out on the bed beside her. She bit her lip. 'It's not just sex?'

'Every time we made love I told you with my body what my brain was too stubborn to accept,' Carlos said deeply. He held her hand over his heart. 'Feel what you do to me, *mi corazón*. My heart beats for you.'

His hands shook as he traced them over every dip and curve of her body. He feathered kisses over her breasts and his breath grazed her inner thighs as his caresses became ever more erotic. And when he lifted himself over her and possessed her, with a bone-shaking tenderness and a possessiveness that thrilled her, Carlos told her in the language of lovers that he would worship her always and for ever.

EPILOGUE

'You are a miracle-worker,' Betsy told her husband of two years.

They had recently celebrated their second wedding anniversary with a romantic weekend in Mallorca.

'We can go anywhere in the world,' Carlos had said when he'd suggested the trip. 'The best hotel or a luxury cruise ship. You choose.'

'I choose Casita Viola. We never did get around to making love on the beach.'

Carlos had taken care of that, and had made love to her with such dedication that she had felt she loved him even more, if that was possible.

'What miracle have I performed?' he murmured now, as he came over to where she was standing by the window in her art studio. He slid his arms around her waist and pulled her against his chest, his lips nuzzling her ear.

She pointed to the garden, where her parents were each pushing a pram up and down the lawn. 'Mum and Dad have been here for three days and they haven't argued once. They even get on with each other's new partners. What did you do?'

'I very cleverly made you pregnant with twins, so that they had a granddaughter each to coo over.' Carlos winced as they watched Sebastian charge across the grass and kick a football, which sailed over the pram where six-month-old Ana-Marta was sleeping. Betsy's mother was pushing the other pram, with baby Alicia inside. 'I don't know where our son gets his energy from.'

'I wonder…' Betsy said drily. 'I can't decide if he is going to be a famous footballer or a tennis champion, but all that matters is that he is happy.' She turned in Carlos's arms and captured his beloved face in her hands. 'Have you any idea how happy you make *me*?'

'I love you.' He kissed her lingeringly. 'I never believed I could be this happy. A beautiful wife and three gorgeous children—what more could I want?'

'How about four gorgeous children?' Betsy grinned at his startled expression. 'All that sex on the beach in Mallorca has given us a lovely surprise.'

Carlos laughed and hugged her tight before he scooped her up and carried her over to the sofa. 'I'm delighted by your news. But how do you feel about falling pregnant so soon after having the twins?'

'I feel that I am the luckiest woman in the world. You are my world, Carlos. You and our children. My parents, your father, Graciela and Miguel, Chico… It's my dream come true. Family.'

'For ever,' he said softly, before he kissed her. 'By the way, I have locked the door, *querida,* and you will have my undivided attention.'

* * * * *

Unable to put Housekeeper in the Headlines *down? Find your next page-turner with these other stories by Chantelle Shaw!*

Reunited by a Shock Pregnancy
Wed for the Spaniard's Redemption
Proof of Their Forbidden Night
Her Wedding Night Negotiation

Available now!

WE HOPE YOU ENJOYED
THIS BOOK FROM
⟨H⟩HARLEQUIN

PRESENTS

Escape to exotic locations where passion knows no bounds.

Welcome to the glamorous lives of royals and billionaires, where passion knows no bounds. Be swept into a world of luxury, wealth and exotic locations.

8 NEW BOOKS AVAILABLE EVERY MONTH!

#3861 THE RULES OF HIS BABY BARGAIN
by Louise Fuller
Casino mogul Charlie Law promised his dying father he'd find his infant half brother and bring him home. He didn't allow for the baby's aunt and guardian, beautiful Dora Thorn, to counter his every move!

#3862 INNOCENT IN THE SHEIKH'S PALACE
by Dani Collins
Plain librarian Hannah Meeks decided to start the family she's desperately wanted—on her own. Only to discover that her miracle baby is actually the heir to Sheikh Akin Sarraf's desert throne...

#3863 PLAYING THE BILLIONAIRE'S GAME
by Pippa Roscoe
Fourteen days. That's how long exiled Duke Sebastian gives art valuer Sia Keating to prove he stole a famous painting. And how long she'll have to avoid the pull of embracing their dangerous attraction...

#3864 THE VOWS HE MUST KEEP
The Avelar Family Scandals
by Amanda Cinelli
Tycoon Valerio Marchesi swore to keep Daniela Avelar safe. Discovering she's in grave danger, he insists she becomes his bride! But their engagement of convenience is a red-hot fire burning out of control!

HPCNMRB1020

*The hottest actor in Bollywood, Vikram Raawal has
found love countless times—on-screen. In real life, he's
given up on finding a soul-deep connection. Until at a
masquerade ball, shy assistant Naina Menon leaves him
craving more…*

*Read on for a sneak preview of
Tara Pammi's next story for Harlequin Presents,*
Claiming His Bollywood Cinderella.

The scent of her hit him first. A subtle blend of jasmine and
her that he'd remember for the rest of his life. And equate
with honesty and irreverence and passion and laughter. There
was a joy about this woman, despite her insecurities and
vulnerabilities, that he found almost magical.

The mask she wore was black satin with elaborate gold
threading at the edges and was woven tightly into her hair,
leaving just enough of her beautiful dark brown eyes visible. The
bridge of her small nose was revealed as was the slice of her
cheekbones. For a few seconds, Vikram had the overwhelming
urge to tear it off. He wanted to see her face. Not because he
wanted to find out her identity.

He wanted to see her face because he wanted to know this
woman. He wanted to know everything about her. He wanted…
With a rueful shake of his head, he pushed away the urge. It was
more than clear that men had only ever disappointed her. He was
damned if he was going to be counted as one of them. He wanted
to be different in her memory.

When she remembered him after tonight, he wanted her to smile. He wanted her to crave more of him. Just as he would crave more of her. He knew this before their lips even touched. And he would find a way to discover her identity. He was just as sure of that, too.

Her mouth was completely uncovered. Her lipstick was mostly gone, leaving a faint pink smudge that he wanted to lick away with his tongue.

She held the edge of her silk dress with one hand, and as she lifted it to move, he got a flash of a thigh. Soft and smooth and silky. It was like receiving a jolt of electricity with every inch he discovered of this woman. The dress swooped low in the front, baring the upper curves of her breasts in a tantalizing display.

And then there she was, within touching distance. Sitting with her legs folded beneath her, looking straight into his eyes. One arm held the sofa while the other smoothed repeatedly over the slight curve of her belly. She was nervous and he found it both endearing and incredibly arousing. She wanted to please herself. And him. And he'd never wanted more for a woman to discover pleasure with him.

Her warm breath hit him somewhere between his mouth and jaw in silky strokes that resonated with his heartbeat. This close, he could see the tiny scar on the other corner of her mouth.

"Are you going to do anything?" she asked after a couple of seconds, sounding completely put out.

He wanted to laugh and tug that pouty lower lip with his teeth. Instead he forced himself to take a breath. He was never going to smell jasmine and not think of her ever again. "It's your kiss, darling. You take it."

Don't miss
Claiming His Bollywood Cinderella,
available November 2020 wherever
Harlequin Presents books and ebooks are sold.

Harlequin.com